STONE SONG

THE ISLE OF DESTINY SERIES BOOK 1

TRICIA O'MALLEY

LOVEWRITE PUBLISHING

Stone Song

The Isle of Destiny Series

Book 1

Copyright © 2016 by Lovewrite Publishing
All Rights Reserved

Cover Design:
Rebecca Frank Cover Designs
Editor:
Elayne Morgan

Dedicated to those who aren't afraid to look for magick.

"Those who do not believe in magic will never find it." – *Roald Dahl*

CHAPTER 1

"'*A*nd you, Children of Danu, shall go to the land of which shall be called Inisfail, the Isle of Destiny. It is your destiny to populate the earth and bring to it the great wisdom and direction that you have learned under our hands,'" Bianca intoned as Clare rolled her eyes and winked at her roommate, who was giving a mythological tour of Dublin to a group of eager Americans. "Look now, there goes one of the great beauties of the Children of Danu. A living goddess herself."

The group turned to stare at Clare as she rushed past them, shaking her head at Bianca.

"I'm as much of a goddess as you are a delicate rose," Clare shot back, and the group broke out in laughter.

"And so the children of Danu came to the Isle of Destiny, which you know today as Ireland, with only the four treasures in their hands to protect them against those who were determined to rule the island in darkness."

Bianca's mythology lesson faded behind Clare as she tucked a rioting mass of auburn curls under a wool cap, her mind already focused on her dissertation project. It was her last bit of work to be finished before she could call herself an honest-to-god doctor.

A person with a geology doctorate is nonetheless a doctor, she reminded herself as she pushed through the glass doors that housed the science wing of Trinity College.

She'd been lucky to get accepted to the reciprocal geology program at such an esteemed college, and even luckier to have won a full scholarship. Her parents had scratched their heads in confusion – wondering what a farmer's daughter from small-town Clifden, Ireland would want with a doctorate degree.

To study stones, no less.

She could still see her father striding out into the yard, his boots mucked with mud, as he bent over and picked up a rock from the ground and held it up to the light.

"This? This is what you're wanting to be studying then? Sure and there isn't all that much to learn about them now, is there?"

Though he'd been confused by her choice, Madden MacBride had quickly been found boasting about his brilliant daughter in Paddy's, the corner pub he favored.

Clare still remembered her first moments of panic when her parents had dropped her off in the city, their truck rumbling away from the college, looking conspicuously out of place next to the slick cars that cluttered the busy streets of Dublin. As she'd glanced down at her worn denim pants and faded button-down shirt, she'd imagined that she looked much like the dilapidated truck she'd been dropped off by.

The better to dig in the dirt, she'd reminded herself and had lifted her chin high as she'd returned to the apartment she'd rented with a girl from a list the college had provided her with. And even though they'd spoken a few times on the telephone over the summer, she'd still felt like her stomach was twisted in knots as she'd waited for her new roomie to arrive.

It had taken less than thirty seconds, and one glance at the tears streaming down the chubby blonde's face, before Clare had instantly bonded with Bianca.

They'd lived together ever since, graduating to a slightly better apartment, slightly better fashion-sense, and the worldly air that comes with finally navigating a city as an adult.

Bianca, who'd majored in history with a minor in mythology, was currently in a year-long debate with herself over whether or not to pursue her doctorate. In the meantime, she worked full-time in the National Museum of Ireland, and part-time as a tour guide for those who had a yen to learn some of the Celtic myths that wound their way through Ireland's rich history.

Though Clare's scholarship covered her tuition, she still needed some extra cash for certain essentials – like the camera she'd been eyeing for eons, and a full Irish breakfast after her nights out on the town with Bianca. Clare supplemented her income by working one or two nights a week at a pub down the street from their flat, and a few afternoons a week at a local crystal shop.

Crystals were rocks, after all. Geodes, if she was going to get specific.

Clare winced as she thought about her second job. She couldn't really say how she'd ended up walking past the crystal shop one sunny fall day, but the pretty display of glittering stones had drawn her eye. Artfully arranged on varying tiers of lucite towers, interspersed with delicate jewelry and a few books, the window display managed to be both fanciful and tasteful in the same breath.

Unable to resist, Clare had found herself stepping inside. Her skin had hummed with the energy pulsing from the crystals, and the warm lights and the bright smile of the woman standing behind the counter had made her feel like she was being welcomed home.

It annoyed Clare that to this day she couldn't figure out why stones spoke to her. Well, not literally talked to her, but she knew each of their signature energies, could tell what they needed or who they needed to be with, and could even gauge where they'd come from with just a glance.

Sure, some of that was a result of her education. What was she getting a geology degree for if she couldn't eye up a stone and estimate its age? But the energy and the power of stones? Well, she'd yet to understand how she could physically feel that.

Not that she'd brought it up to any of her professors.

Getting an education in a scientific field – especially as a woman – didn't much lend itself to flights of fancy. Instead, she'd proven herself to be a rational, brilliant, and committed scientist. Once a week, Clare taught an under-graduate class that was well attended – though some would say that was because the teacher was hot.

Clare snorted at the thought as she pushed open the door to the science wing and waved at the girl working the front desk.

It mattered little what you looked like when you were knee-deep in the bog, pulling out stones to be analyzed. The sooner her students realized that looks weren't neces-sarily a benefit in this field of study, the better off they'd be.

"Hey Seamus," Clare called to the lab attendant as she entered the small lab dedicated to her field of study. Not that rocks and the formation of the earth weren't an inter-esting branch of science – but Clare knew that the biomedical engineers and chemists rated much better labs on the top floor of the science building, not to mention better funding. Sometimes she felt like they'd sequestered her department to the far recesses of the dungeon.

"Still blustering out?" Seamus called easily, popping a mint in his mouth as he crossed his wiry arms over his chest and leaned back in the chair. At six feet tall, he was all arms and elbows, with a crop of dark hair that stuck up all over his head. He made up for his lankiness with an effortlessly cool street style.

"Misting at best, I'd say. Bianca had a group out, so

not all that bad," Clare said as she pulled her knapsack off and hung it on the back of her chair.

"Ah, maybe I should go say hi," Seamus said, a blush tinging his cheeks. "She still dating that Conor?"

Clare glanced up at him. "Nah, she's given him the boot after him staying out all night with his band a few weeks ago."

Seamus straightened, his feet hitting the floor with a thud.

"Maybe I *should* go say hi. Just, you know, to catch up with her," Seamus mumbled as he grabbed his coat and hit the door at almost a run.

Clare chuckled as she put her ear buds in and fired up her computer.

Her dissertation wasn't going to write itself.

CHAPTER 2

"*D*on't you have to work at the shop today?"

Clare started as Seamus tugged the ear bud from her ear, the wail of Jimi Hendrix's guitar sounding from the tiny speaker as it dropped to the table in front of her.

"Shite, shite, shite, you're right," Clare swore. "I got caught up. I need to run." She made sure to save her work, double-checked saving it on her jump drive, and checked saving it to her cloud account one more time before she jumped up.

"Come have a pint later," Clare said, pausing to buss her lips across Seamus's cheek.

"Are you at O'Flannery's too, then?"

"No, come by our place. You want to see Bianca, don't you?"

Clare didn't wait for his answer as she breezed out the door and headed for the crystal shop. She knew that one of these days she would need to get better at managing her time, but it was so difficult for her to turn her mind off when she was engrossed in a subject.

Not that Branna minded all that much when she was a few minutes late. Among Branna's employees, Clare held the highest record for sales, so Branna was content to give Clare some leniency on her hours.

Celtic Crystals was located about a fifteen-minute walk from Trinity College, tucked on a windy cobblestone side street. A few shops surrounded it, but for the most part, the shop was fairly isolated from the street traffic – which is why it was a constant surprise to Clare that the store did a steady stream of business.

She had to admit, though, there was something entirely welcoming and, well, dare she say almost magickal about the shop. Clare pulled the cap from her hair as she pushed the door open, the small wind chimes affixed to the door letting out a gentle tinkling welcome sound.

"I'm sorry I'm late," Clare immediately called as she shook out her curls and tucked her cap in the pocket of her shearling-lined canvas coat.

Branna smiled at her from where she stood with a customer by a shelf containing some intricate amethyst chunks. At fifty years of age, Branna could easily pass for years younger; few lines marred her smooth skin and her mass of dark curls hung almost to her waist. Silver and gold bangles clamored for space at her wrists, necklaces strung with crystals lined her throat, and pretty peridot earrings winked at her ears. Branna waved Clare on easily and continued her discussion with the customer.

Breathing a sigh of relief, Clare hung her coat and knapsack in the back room and poured herself a cup of tea from the electric kettle that was just beginning to boil in the back room. Without fail, Branna always had water ready for a cup of tea for Clare.

Clare cupped her hands around a mug with the Celtic Crystals logo etched daintily on its side, and moved toward her nook in the front room. Part of the appeal of Celtic Crystals was that it wasn't set up like a typical store. Instead, the shop was painted a rich honey color and divided into little conversation nooks and crannies, each area offering a place for someone to sit down, pick up a book, or pass the time with a cup of tea while looking at pretty stones. There were no glass-fronted display cases, no signs that said 'please do not touch,' and not even a checkout counter to be found. Instead, a small cabinet next to an armchair in a corner held all the equipment, bags, and boxes that the customers needed. When a customer was ready to check out, Clare would wrap their purchases in pretty purple tissue paper and silver bags bearing the store's logo, and run their credit cards on a small hand-held device.

Just because the shop looked whimsical didn't mean that Branna wasn't up on all the latest technology. Clare credited their steady sales to the highly engaged customer base that Branna maintained interactions with on Instagram and Facebook.

Clare settled into her armchair, the worn leather enveloping her, and she felt herself begin to relax an inch at a time as the warm spell of the shop drifted over her. It was hard to be stressed out over her dissertation – or pretty much anything else in life – when she was in this store. It seemed to say, here, lay your problems at the door and just relax for a while.

Which was one of the reasons she continued to work here. It was so far from her highly regimented schooling that it was almost like going to a yoga class every after-noon. Or so she thought – not like she'd ever taken a yoga class. Clare rolled her eyes at the thought as she began to flip through the inventory folder to make note of what they would need to order soon.

"I got you a gift," Branna said, and Clare tilted her head to look up at her smiling boss.

"A gift? For being late all the time? Well, I'll just have to be coming in later and later each day then," Clare teased.

"Because everyone deserves gifts sometimes," Branna said easily, pulling two small boxes from behind her back. One was beautifully wrapped in silver paper shot through with specks of gold. The other was just a plain white box.

"Wow, like real gifts. Which one should I open first?" Clare asked.

"You choose," Branna said, a smile dancing across her pretty face.

Deciding to save the best for last, Clare opened the small white box and snorted out a laugh.

"Eye shadow?"

"Oh yes, they were having a sale on just the loveliest shades. I couldn't help but get myself one in every color," Branna gushed.

Clare smiled up at her. "Sure, with your gray eyes you can pretty much wear any color. But, um, purple? For me?"

"Well, it's really more of a deep plum, isn't it? Trust me, just a light touch of this and those emerald green eyes of yours will pop."

"Like I need them to pop any more than they do?" Clare asked. It was true, too. Her eyes were the feature people commented on most, and next up was the riot of deep auburn curls on her head.

"Trust me on this one. Just try it out. It would do you some good to primp once in a while."

"Are you saying I'm not stylish enough? I think I'm doing better than I once was," Clare pointed out.

"You're lovely, inside and out. But a woman should use all the tools in her toolbox, if you get what I'm saying."

Clare shook her head and laughed at her boss as she began to peel the paper away from the other gift. She paused as she began to feel the thrum of power that radiated from inside. With a curious glance for Branna, she returned to peeling the paper gently off the box.

They hadn't spoken much about Clare's intuition with stones. Branna seemed to recognize it, but gave Clare her space on the subject. It just wasn't something that she was comfortable talking about – with anyone.

Clare gasped as she opened the box.

"Why, Branna, it's quite lovely, it is at that," Clare murmured as she pulled the necklace gently from the box. Hung on a smooth silver strand was an intricate Celtic knot, twisted into four loops with an intersecting circle. Clare now understood where the pulse of power came from. Hung suspended in the middle of the knot was a small but fiercely polished sphere of nuummite.

"The Sorcerer's Stone," Clare murmured.

"I thought the symbol would resonate with you as well," Branna said, tilting her head at Clare, a knowing look in her gray eyes.

Clare held the pendant up so that it dangled in front of her face.

"It's just a Celtic knot, right? I mean, it has the circle connecting the four corners, so that's somewhat unusual, but otherwise, it's pretty traditional, eh?"

Branna said nothing, just smiled gently and pressed her hand to Clare's shoulder as she turned to greet the next customer already walking through the door. Clare wasn't about to admit that the symbol had left her shaken. For what reason? She considered the design of the knot and the pretty stone that swung in its middle. It wasn't like she hadn't been around nuummite before. It was a fairly popular – and fairly powerful – stone, though far be it from her to actually admit to anyone that it emitted its own pulse of energy. It was one thing to talk up the legend of a stone for sales – and entirely another thing to admit that she had a very real and visceral reaction to the stone held in her hand.

As she stared at the Celtic knot, a low pulse of something, almost as if she wanted to scratch an itch, pressed against the nape of her neck. Annoyed, Clare rubbed her finger over the spot.

"Clare, could you assist Mrs. Miller with her order? I've just got to finish this internet order that I've started."

No time for fanciful daydreams, Clare thought, but she slipped the necklace over her head anyway, as it was a gift from Branna. The charm settled between her breasts, the metal cool against her skin, its touch both intimate and unsettling.

And Clare swore she could feel the heat of the stone, dead center in the necklace, pulsing gently near her heart.

CHAPTER 3

The weather conditions hadn't improved by the time Clare finished closing the shop, counting the till, and putting in the inventory order. Not atypically for a January night in Dublin, the wind whipped down the alley and threatened to snatch her wool cap from her head. Clare tugged it down lower and huddled into her coat, keeping her eyes on the slick pavement in front of her as she hustled to get home before the dampness soaked straight to her core.

It wasn't all that surprising that the streets still bustled with activity. A bit of wind and rain did little to keep people from their evening pints at the pub. A warm glow of light spilled from the front window of a pub and Clare caught a glimpse of a pretty woman laughing next to a man who was tuning the strings on a fiddle. It was a cozy scene and almost made Clare itch to go in for a pint.

Until the man's eyes shifted to molten silver and met hers through the glass.

The moment hung suspended between them as Clare gasped for breath, the wind pummeling into her and whipping her curls across her face. When she pushed the hair back from her eyes, the man was just a man, his dark brown eyes gleaming in the light of the small fire next to him. Calling out, he lifted the fiddle to his shoulder and began to play, a chorus of voices rising to meet his.

Tossing her hair, Clare turned and pressed against the increasingly insistent wind, her head bowed as she tried to shake the chill that had come over her – a chill that had nothing to do with the weather. The necklace, still strung around her neck, seemed to burn into her skin. Digging into her coat, Clare grabbed the pendant and held it up, and gasped when she saw that the little stone dangling in the middle seemed to glow in the dull light of the streetlamp.

Had she not gotten enough sleep last night? She knew she was stressed – wasn't every graduate student stressed? Between the pressures of school, holding down several jobs, and still trying to maintain a semblance of a social life, Clare wasn't exactly taking the best care of herself. She would let herself sleep in tomorrow, she decided, and hopefully the extra hours of shut-eye would stave off any further weird instances of glowing silver eyes.

Her body gave an involuntary shudder as she thought about the man in the pub again.

Clare pushed her way through the wind, turning down a side street that wound its way to her building. Hurrying now, the sounds of the busier part of the city fading, she felt the hair on the back of her neck stand up. With a jolt, she whipped around and stared at the empty street behind her. For a moment, her eyes searched the areas where the light didn't quite reach – crevices behind dumpsters, shadows cast by buildings. Was someone following her?

Finding nothing, Clare turned and ran headlong into a brick wall.

Or at least so it felt.

Clare shrieked as she realized that the wall was in fact a man – a very muscular, very leather-clad, and very menacing-looking man. Bringing her knapsack around, she moved to swing it at his head and gasped as he deflected her, his arm wrapping around her waist as he swung her behind him.

Shielding her.

Clare froze as the man's arm struck out, a silver dagger gleaming in his hand an instant before it sliced through the person who'd appeared virtually from nowhere behind her. Clare choked as the dagger slid through the heart of the silver-eyed man from the pub. Her breath caught, and she squeaked as the man slipped to the ground in a puddle of liquid silver light before vanishing completely from sight.

Locked in place by a muscular arm, Clare's entire body began to shake as she tried to process what she had just seen.

"I think I'm going to be sick," she finally gasped, and the arm released her. She stumbled forward a few feet and bent at the waist, retching a little. But only stomach bile came up; she hadn't eaten in hours. Wiping her mouth on the back of her hand, Clare turned, faint trembles still shivering through her, and faced the unknown.

"Better?" His voice, like a razor blade dipped in honey, sliced through her core.

"Who... what are you? What is this?" Clare's voice shook, but she stood straighter, looking around the alley for any other attackers.

"I'm your Protector," the man said simply.

Clare tilted her head in question, her mouth dropping open. She gaped for a moment, but no words came.

"And you shouldn't be walking down dark streets alone at night," the man continued, pulling out a rag to clean the blade of his dagger before sliding the knife into his waistband. Clare's eyebrows rose.

"Excuse me?" she finally said as she studied him.

The man easily had a foot of height on her, his shoulders so broad he could have been a rugby player, and the leather coat he wore hugged his muscles like a second skin. Fitted jeans, dark boots, and midnight hair just long enough to tousle in the wind completed the look. Everything on him was sharp – and the energy radiating from him was like a tightly coiled spring. Only when he angled his face into the light did she see that his eyes were a distinct and almost startling blue.

Black Irish, Clare thought dumbly.

"You should be paying better attention to your surroundings. Especially in this time."

"I have no idea what you're talking about – nor do I

know what you mean by 'in this time.' This time at night? Why, it's not quite half nine in the evening. That's positively early for a Dubliner," Clare scoffed.

A brief hint of a smile crossed his handsome face, the flash of his teeth slicing through the craggy features.

"Your turn. Your time. Four months," the man elaborated.

"Sure and you haven't been drinking this evening?" Clare asked, making no sense of his words. Her mind still scrambled to process what she'd seen on the street.

"No, no drinks for me this evening." A ghost of a smile crossed his face again.

"Nice dagger. Care to tell me about that little magick trick you just pulled?" Clare asked, gesturing to where she'd have sworn she'd just seen a man melt into the pavement in a silvery puddle.

The man studied her for a moment and then turned and let out a stream of curses that echoed down the empty street. Turning back, he looked at her, those blue eyes burning into hers.

"You don't know, do you?"

Clare shook her head at him, raising her hands in confusion.

"Go home." The man cursed again, turning to leave.

"Wait." Clare jumped forward, surprising herself by grabbing his arm. Hot waves of energy seemed to pulse beneath her hand and she dropped it. "What's your name? What do you mean you're my Protector?"

The man sighed and ran his hands over the stubble on

his jaw, turning to look back over his shoulder at her, his eyes searing her to the spot.

"Call me Blake. Stay out of dark corners, Miss MacBride."

And with that, he disappeared as quickly as he had appeared, leaving Clare staring at the empty street and wondering briefly if she'd been drugged.

It didn't stop her from running the entire rest of the way home.

CHAPTER 4

*B*lake followed Clare from a distance, slipping from shadow to shadow, his movements silent and precise. He knew every dip and curve, every hiding spot along this route to her home. He'd walked it for years.

He refused to let himself think about the fact that he had been instantly attracted to Clare from the moment he had first seen her years ago. And touching her just now? It was enough to drive him crazy. Blake cursed again. There was no time for dalliances and the distractions they could provide. Not when there was so much at stake.

Blake watched as Clare raced to a brownstone apartment building, nestled in between two mismatched walkups. He waited as she shoved her key in the lock of the front door and in seconds she'd disappeared into the foyer. Blake didn't need to see her to be able to track her as she raced up the stairs to the third floor. If he was within a mile of her, he could sense her exact location – even her mood.

Some would say it was a gift – while others considered it to be a great curse.

All Blake knew was that it was his destiny.

Turning, he made his way to where his Range Rover sat parked in front of Clare's apartment building. Climbing into the back seat, Blake pulled a tattered novel from a bag on the floor and began to read in the faint light of the streetlamp.

It was going to be a long night.

CHAPTER 5

"**W**ell here she is," Bianca exclaimed as Clare blew through the door. Her roommate's cheeks were tinged faintly with pink, and Clare could surmise what had been happening prior to her entrance.

"I'll just grab you a pint then," Seamus said quickly, rising from where he'd been sitting next to Bianca on the small settee in their cramped living room. Bianca smoothed her hands down her rumpled navy skirt and smiled brightly at Clare.

"How was work then? You look a little stressed out," Bianca said, finally zeroing in on the look on Clare's face.

"I... I..." Clare looked at Bianca helplessly, her mouth working as the words struggled to get out. Just what was she going to say, exactly?

"Why, you look like you saw the ghost of ol' Paddy who looms over the hills," Bianca said, rising to cross to

Clare. Seamus pushed back into the room, a can of Guinness in his hand.

"Hey now, what's the problem?" Seamus asked,
concern crossing his face.

"I think she's seen a ghost," Bianca said, dragging a
still wordless Clare across the room and pushing her into a
tweed armchair. Seamus silently handed Clare the can of
Guinness and Clare immediately guzzled it, the cool liquid
soothing away some of the panic that still laced her stomach. She closed her eyes for a moment, allowing the wash
of liquid to hit her empty stomach, praying that it would
stay down. When it did, she finally opened her eyes to
look at her friends.

"A man stopped me from a mugging tonight," Clare
finally said, deciding that she needed a little time to
process everything she had just seen. Plus, if she had
seen something that she wasn't supposed to, the last
thing she wanted to do was drag her favorite people
into it.

"No!" Bianca gasped, settling onto the couch again,
Seamus at her side. Together they leaned forward, their
elbows on their knees, mirroring each other's position.

"Aye, and the man was tall, dark, and handsome too,"
Clare said, knowing that would distract her roomie.

"Ohhhh, that sounds amazing," Bianca breathed and
Seamus sat back, annoyance crossing his handsome
features.

"Seamus, can you get me a scone or a biscuit? My
stomach is really upset," Clare asked, deciding to give her

lab assistant something to do before he stormed off in a huff.

"Tell me everything," Bianca said, her bright blue eyes alive with excitement. Once her fear of Clare being hurt had passed, Bianca was ready to settle into a good story.

"You know he's a liking for you, right?" Clare hissed, pointing her beer at the swinging door to the kitchen.

"Sure and I'd say so – he kissed me right before you burst through the door like the hounds of hell were chasing you," Bianca hissed back.

"Is that a good thing?" Clare asked.

"I'm still making up me mind," Bianca said, then smiled at Seamus as he walked through the door with a plate of biscuits.

"Thanks, Seamus," Clare said, balancing the plate on her leg and eagerly biting into a biscuit. Washing the buttery crumbs down with another sip of her beer, she launched into her story – changing only the parts about the silver puddle, the dagger, and what he had said about protecting her.

"It seemed like he'd been following me, though," Clare said through a mouthful of biscuit. Now that she'd started eating, she was having a hard time not shoveling the biscuits down her throat.

"The mugger? Or the handsome stranger?" Bianca asked while Seamus slid a glance at her.

"The handsome stranger. Blake," Clare said.

"Blake. Sounds hot," Bianca gushed, and Seamus shook his head.

"Listen, I'm going to leave you two. Call me if you need me to walk you to the lab tomorrow," Seamus said, standing up and patting Clare's shoulder lightly as he passed her chair. Clare reached up and grabbed his hand, squeezing it briefly.

"Thanks, friend. I'll let you know."

Seamus paused by the door, his eyes on Bianca as he shoved his hands through his already messy hair.

Clare tilted her head and raised an eyebrow at her roomie.

"Oh, well, yes, Seamus, I'll just see you out then," Bianca said, jumping up quickly and following Seamus out into the hallway.

Clare leaned back in the chair and considered their living room as she waited for Bianca to stop kissing Seamus. A pretty woven rug in colors of mossy green and yellow covered the worn wood floor. The tweed chair she was currently curled up in picked up the same tone of green, and the walls echoed a faded version of the same color. With mismatched prints of the Irish countryside cluttering the walls and pretty lace curtains in the tall windows that ranged the front of the room, it was a cozy and welcoming – if slightly threadbare – room. Bianca and Clare had decided not to spend too much of their money on decorating. Instead, they'd invested their time and energy into updating their wardrobe and doing their best to wash away their country girl looks. Here and there they'd added little touches to the apartment, but for the most part, the girls kept the place uncluttered, sparse, and fairly clean.

Bianca slid back in the front door, a guilty look on her face.

"What? Why do you look so guilty?" Clare demanded.

"He likes me. And you work with him. And I liked kissing him. And… and… I don't know," Bianca wailed and dramatically collapsed on the couch.

Despite herself, Clare found her lips twitching into a smile.

"I like Seamus. You could do far worse," Clare pointed out.

"Yeah, but he's *so* not my type! I mean, he's tall and awkward, and sort of gangly, but when he kisses me?" Bianca fanned her face dramatically as she stared up at their ceiling from the couch. "It all falls away and I just want to jump him."

"So jump him," Clare said with a smile.

Bianca sat up and pushed a lock of blonde hair behind her ear.

"You think? I mean, I should?" Bianca asked, her face serious.

Clare chuckled, taking another swig of her beer. The normalcy of the conversation was beginning to push the weird events she'd experienced earlier to the back of her mind.

"I think you should do whatever you feel like doing. But, here's a suggestion, maybe let him woo you a bit first."

"Woo me?" Bianca said in the same tone as if she'd just spotted a cockroach.

"Yes, woo you. You're always so quick to fall head over heels in love with the wrong guy. Why don't you just let it unfold naturally?"

Bianca blinked her blue eyes at Clare, an expression of awe dawning on her face.

"Woo me, she says. Woo me," Bianca muttered to herself, as though the concept was entirely foreign to her.

"Yes, woo you! Give him the chance to take you out to dinner. That kind of thing. He's been watching you for a long time, you know. Asking after you," Clare said.

"He has not!" Bianca all but squealed, her eyes dagger-sharp as she narrowed them at Clare. "You've said not a thing. Not one thing."

Clare shrugged. "It wasn't for me to say. You were always involved. Now you're not."

"Seamus." Bianca shook her head, bringing her fingers to her lips. "I'd never considered Seamus. He is quite cute though, isn't he?"

"And he's a good guy," Clare agreed.

"Enough about him. Tell me more about this handsome stranger." Bianca waved it away and then jumped up. "Hold on. I'll be getting us another pint for this round."

Clare smiled and stretched her feet out, the shock of her earlier encounter beginning to fade away in the warm glow of her living room and the cheerful banter with her roommate.

Bianca breezed back in with a bottle of Middleton and two whiskey glasses.

"I think whiskey is in order," Bianca declared, setting one glass down by Clare and pouring her a generous splash. Clare picked up the glass and studied the amber liquid before she held it up in salute to her roomie.

"*Sláinte.*"

"Now, tell me why you think he was following you," Bianca demanded, bringing Clare right back into the confusion and fear she'd felt an hour ago.

Clare pressed her lips together as she considered just how much to tell Bianca.

"He said something like… 'you don't know?' And something about protecting me," Clare finally said, taking a small sip of the whiskey, enjoying the burn of it as it settled in the pit of her stomach.

Bianca fanned her face dramatically again.

"Protecting you! A mysterious handsome stranger sent to protect you. It's like a fairytale!" Bianca gushed, her enthusiasm radiating through her.

Leave it to Bianca to jump right to fairytales and legends. This was right up her alley, Clare thought, as she took another sip of her whiskey. Speaking of…

"You wouldn't know anything about silver eyes would you? Er, or anything to do with protection from silvery something or another?" Clare mumbled, before clamping her lips down on the words. It sounded just as ridiculous as it had seemed in her head.

"Well, silver eyes would be fae," Bianca said automatically, then scrunched up her pert nose as she thought. "But I'd have to look up the protection thing. I'm certain I've heard various stories regarding protection spells or protectors. You know me, I've loads of mythology books."

Fae.

Clare's heart had skipped a beat at that word. Of course, living in Ireland came with reams of myths and legends regarding the fae. It was as interwoven in their history as any other religious legends and stories. But she'd never been one to give the legends any weight or credence.

And yet here she sat, pondering a silvery glow seen in an unknown stranger's eyes, and trying desperately to tamp down her curiosity over the man whose arm had held her so tightly pressed to his body.

Protecting her from the unknown.

CHAPTER 6

*B*lake.

He'd haunted her dreams, this mysterious stranger – the protector of herself and the warrior of the unknown.

Clare stumbled blurry-eyed into her shower, letting the warm stream of water wash away the remnants of the dream that still tangled her thoughts. It would do little good to obsess over the unknown, Clare thought as she grabbed her favorite citrus-scented bath gel. She was a scientist, wasn't she? When presented with a question she couldn't answer – she researched it.

Clare grumbled her way through her morning routine, picking out a pair of dark jeans, knee-high brown boots, and a heather green cowl neck sweater that made her eyes pop. As a concession to the weather, she spent some time drying her curls so her hair wouldn't be sopping wet when she stepped outside.

"Damn it, Bianca," Clare hissed when she saw the note on the kitchen counter.

All out of tea and coffee! Sorry, love. I'll pick up extra today. Wanted to get out early to get some research done for you. Call Seamus to walk you to class if you must. Text me.

No tea or coffee? Now Clare would be forced to enter the busy streets of Dublin far sooner than she was willing or wanting to have contact with other people.

"Just brilliant. I'll go to Bee & Bun," Clare said out loud, not really all that upset about being forced to cozy up in her favorite coffee shop this morning.

Thursdays were her easy day of the week. With just an afternoon shift at the crystal shop and no classes to teach, she typically used the extra time for researching or running errands around the city. Ever precise, Clare jotted a note in her day planner before slipping it into her knapsack next to her laptop.

Research protectors and silver-eyed fae.

It looked a little ridiculous, one line down from her note about contacting an institute in London regarding a study on seismic shifts she'd been meaning to read. Rolling her eyes at herself, Clare zipped the bag closed and reached for her coat. Not needing to check the weather to know she'd need a coat and her cap, she tugged both on and stepped from her apartment, taking extra care to lock up and look around. There would be no popping in her headphones and listening to music on her stroll this morning. Even if she didn't fully understand what had happened last night, she wasn't stupid.

It would be smart to keep her wits about her.

Pushing the foyer door open, Clare poked her head out and looked both ways down the street. Aside from a mother pushing her pram down the street, it was empty. Which wasn't unusual for nine in the morning on a Thursday. Seeing nothing that could be viewed as an immediate threat, Clare turned left and headed toward her favorite morning coffee spot.

The sun struggled to peek through a blanket of heavy gray clouds, and a slight breeze kicked up her hair. As far as Clare was concerned, this was grand weather for a January morning. If she was lucky, she might even have to pull her sunglasses out of her bag.

Clare hummed to herself so as to appear nonchalant, but she was on full alert as her eyes scanned every pedestrian she came across. By the time she'd reached Bee & Bun, Clare began to feel a little ridiculous. Not a single person had exhibited silver eyes or fairy wings or anything else that could remotely be construed as out of the ordinary. Aside from the homeless man on the corner holding up a torch and declaring that the end of the world was near.

But that wasn't really all that odd.

Clare tugged her hat off her head as she stepped into Bee & Bun, the warm scents of vanilla and cinnamon enveloping her as she slid past crowded tables to the long glass displays toward the back of the restaurant.

"Looking gorgeous as always," said Cian, one half of the delightfully gay couple who owned the coffee shop, as Clare approached the counter.

"Sure and it's nice to hear that. I slept for shite, that's for certain." Clare smiled at him.

"Still gorgeous," Cian said, raising an eyebrow at her. "The usual?"

"Espresso today. And scrambled eggs and toast. I missed dinner last night."

"I'll just bring you a full Irish. I saved your table in back," Cian said, gesturing to where the coffee shop curved to a small alcoved back room that boasted a quieter study area, a small couch, and a tiny gas fireplace. It was prime real estate in the coffee shop, but once Cian had realized that Clare tipped well and would come in almost every Thursday, he began saving it for her.

"You're a god among men." Clare blew him a kiss as she breezed toward her spot.

"Be sure to tell my better half that. He likes to think *he's* the god," Cian quipped, making Clare chuckle as she stopped at her table.

Choosing the corner chair so her back was to the wall and she could look out, Clare let out a sigh of relief when Cian buzzed over with her espresso almost immediately.

"Figured you'd want this straight out. I'll bring water along in a bit."

"You're the best."

Bee & Bun was one of those places that combined modern elegance and cozy charm. It had established itself as not your typical Irish place for tea – all the tables and chairs had sleek lines and monochromatic colors. This was immediately offset by the bright cushions on every chair and the smattering of abstract artwork across the walls. Clare sighed as she sunk into her cushiony seat, blowing first on her espresso before taking a small sip.

Once the caffeine began to hum through her system, Clare fired up her laptop and opened a new document. Considering what to call it, she finally typed a headline.

Fae Research.

Deleting the title quickly, Clare typed in *F&P Research* instead. There, that was better. She sipped her espresso and considered where to start.

"Protein for you," Cian slid a steaming plate of scrambled eggs, perfectly toasted wheat bread, and a collection of jams onto her table. Clare grinned at him and dug into the food as she began to pull up Celtic mythology sites.

"No, that's certainly not it," Clare grumbled as she began reading one legend. Checking the index, she gasped at the sheer number of stories cataloged on the site. Certainly there couldn't be this many legends?

No wonder Bianca was getting her masters in this stuff. One could spend years combing through all the information contained on this site alone.

"Clare? Clare MacBride?"

Clare jumped at her name and looked up from her laptop to see an old woman with pure white hair falling past her shoulders, snapping brown eyes, and a smile that made Clare instantly want to pour out all of her troubles.

"Yes, that's me. Can I be helping you?" Clare asked pleasantly, figuring the woman must have come into the crystal shop at some point. Judging from the stones that hung around her neck and the multitude of bangles that covered her arms, this woman was no stranger to crystals.

"Ah, well, I believe I'm the one that's to be helping you," the woman said. She gestured to the man at her side, who stepped closer and nodded once at Clare. "This is John, the love of my life."

Clare studied the couple for a moment, raising an eyebrow at the comment about love. It certainly was an odd way to introduce someone.

"Have we met?" Clare finally asked, her nerves kicking up a bit. The man smiled kindly at her, his tweed vest and neatly pressed slacks giving him an air of aristocracy while his eyes shone with life and humor.

"I'm sorry, I was just so excited to find you." The woman gestured to the seats across from Clare. "May we sit?"

"I suppose?" Clare left the sentence as a question, so as to hint that she might not be all that thrilled at having company.

"Need any tea?" Cian asked, popping by their table.

"A pot would be good. And a hint of the Irish too," the woman said, unwrapping a woven scarf in heathered greens, and tucking it over the back of her seat.

Clare settled back after pushing her laptop closed, and crossed her arms over her chest.

"Now, now, don't give me that look. You'll want to hear what I have to say." The woman laughed.

"Shall we start with your name?"

"Ah, yes, my apologies. I'm Fiona O'Brien, and this delightful man is my love, John O'Brien."

Clare found herself warming to Fiona, as the woman was clearly besotted with her husband. A part of her hoped she'd experience that same type of love in her lifetime.

"And I'm Clare MacBride, as you seem to be knowing already," Clare said. She paused as Cian busied himself with setting a squat navy teapot in the center of the table and all the accoutrements in a neat little tray on the side.

"Anything else?"

"I think we're good here," Clare said and shot him a smile before turning her gaze back to Fiona. John had yet to offer anything to say, so it seemed that the woman was running the show.

"Yes, I have to apologize for approaching you in this manner. But I've only recently learned that we are in a bit of a time crunch here, so I thought it best to find you as quickly as possible," Fiona said, turning the pot of tea a few times, but not pouring it. A good Irishwoman always lets the tea steep.

"Well, now, you've found me. What can I do for you?" Clare asked again.

"Yes, so it seems," Fiona said, tilting her head and eyeing Clare. For a moment, Clare could have sworn that she felt a brush of energy – similar to the energy that pulsed from stones – wash over her.

"What was that?" Clare demanded, and Fiona raised an eyebrow before a delighted smile split her face.

"Ah, so you do have power then. You are the right one."

Clare glanced around and then leaned forward.

"I'm not sure what you mean by power, but I'll ask you to not speak loudly. I come here often."

"What do you know about your family?" Fiona countered, finally picking up the pot of tea and pouring a cup for herself and John. Clare still had espresso in her cup and she waved the offer of tea away.

"They're simple people, from Clifden. Are they in trouble?" Clare asked, worry beginning to seep through her.

"No, none that I'm aware of. I suppose I should say – your ancestral history."

"None other than that the MacBrides are a proud Irish family descended from the likes of Grace O'Malley herself. Though we've lost much of her grandeur over the years, we're still proud people," Clare said, shrugging one shoulder.

"Ah, yes, that makes us cousins of sorts." Fiona smiled at her again and sipped her tea.

"Is that right? Ah, I see why you've come to find me then. Doing some genealogy, are you? Well, I've not much to add to the story: I'm pursuing my doctorate in geology at Trinity College and have lived in Dublin for a while now." Clare was no longer nervous. It wasn't unheard of to have long-lost relatives seek out a family member across the island. The country wasn't all that big, after all.

"I find it interesting that you're pursuing a degree in geology. Does that mean you know about the treasure then?"

Okay, so maybe she wasn't here to study family genealogy.

"Excuse me? Treasure? I'm sure you've found the wrong person. If there were treasure to be found, I wouldn't have had to apply for scholarships and work three jobs." Clare laughed and tucked a curl behind her ear. "Treasure." She shook her head and picked up her espresso for another drink.

Fiona glanced at John before leveling a look across the table at Clare. It made her want to squirm – as though she were about to be scolded by a schoolteacher.

"Why do you think it is that you can feel the power of stones?" Fiona asked point-blank, and Clare choked on her espresso. She coughed into her napkin, her eyes tearing up for a moment as she caught her breath and tried to gather herself. Who was this woman and how did she know Clare's secret?

"I'm a healer, myself. And I've got a wide range of my own abilities. Like picking thoughts from your mind when I feel like it," Fiona said easily, smiling at Clare over her cup of tea.

Clare glanced around the coffee shop before lowering her face toward the table.

"Could you please keep your voice down? And someone must have told you this...this story about me."

Fiona just looked at Clare patiently.

"I know it because I can read it on you. You also picked up on the brush of my power when I scanned your mind. You're quite powerful. More so than you realize. Tell me, what do you know of *Na Sirtheoir* – the Seekers?"

"*Na Sirtheoir*? I'm not sure I'm following," Clare said, shaking her head in confusion.

But something had shifted inside of her, like a phoenix, stepping from its nest of ashes and standing to flap its brilliantly colored wings. Her stomach began to churn – in angst – in recognition as a spot at her hairline began to throb. Clare reached up and unconsciously rubbed the spot – an area beneath her hairline at the nape of her neck that she was wont to hold tension in. It wasn't unusual for her to find herself rubbing that spot during a particularly difficult exam or after a stressful shift at the pub.

"If not the *Na Sirtheoir*, what about the *Na Cosantoir*?

It felt like the spot on Clare's neck was beginning to sear. She wanted to cry out – whether in pain or joy, she couldn't tell. Fiona's words were tilting her world on its side.

And yet, Clare had no idea why.

"I've not heard of any of these things. What are you doing to me? Why do I feel this way?" Clare hissed across the table.

Fiona reached out and grabbed Clare's arm, her grip surprisingly strong as Clare tried to tug it away. In seconds, though, a cool balm seemed to seep through her, tamping down on the ball of energy that whirled like mad in her stomach. When Fiona released her, Clare pulled her arm back across the table and crossed it over her chest.

"Thank you. For whatever that was," she mumbled.

"You've heard nothing of these two groups? Or the legend?" Fiona continued.

"I... I really have no idea what to say to you. No, I haven't."

"Clare, you're marked. You're *Na Sirtheoir*. The reason you can sense the power of stones is because it is your ultimate destiny to find the one stone. The most powerful of all stones: the Stone of Destiny, the first of the Four Treasures. It's yours to find. Yours to protect. Yours to save from falling into the wrong hands."

It was as though the café had faded away in the background and there was nothing but Fiona – her eyes still kind, but her words forever changing the fabric of Clare's destiny.

Or at least the path she'd thought she'd set in motion for herself.

"I don't know what any of this means. I can't... I can't help you. With this. With any of this. I think you're wrong. I'm not who you think I am," Clare blurted out, suddenly needing to get away from them – from all of this.

"You've a mark. You're branded as one of the *Na Sirtheoir*. It's under your hairline and it throbs when it's trying to tell you something," Fiona said steadily as Clare shook her head.

"No, no I don't."

"Yes, you do. You'll see. Once you go home and take the time to look. You'll see. The thing is… you don't have much time. Too much time has passed already. The stone must be found – and you're the one charged with finding it."

Clare stood up suddenly, her thighs bumping the table and slopping the tea. She grabbed her laptop, not bothering to put it in its case, and snagged her knapsack and coat quickly.

"I've told you already. I'm not who you think I am. Now I'll kindly be asking you to leave me alone," Clare hissed.

"We're staying at the Cherry Hill Hotel. We won't leave until you talk to us," Fiona said.

Clare shook her head again. "No, I won't see you. Please, you're quite possibly a nutter. It's best you seek help." She pushed away from the table, not looking back, barely seeing Cian's shocked face as she raced by him and chucked some euros on the counter.

Fiona's words floated after her, settling like a threat on her shoulders:

"The fate of Ireland rests in your hands."

CHAPTER 7

The fire in Clare's gut burned the entire way to the crystal shop. There was no way what this woman was saying was true – it was obvious she was just angling for a free cup of tea and a warm spot off the blustery street.

Except she hadn't looked homeless.

And the intelligence in her eyes hadn't read crazy to Clare.

The truth of it was, what Fiona'd said had resonated with Clare on a subliminal level that she'd yet to completely understand. But hearing the words – the *Na Sirtheoir* – had felt the way a sword must feel when it slips into its sheath. There was a rightness to it – a realness – that was almost giving Clare a mild panic attack.

She certainly wasn't going to run immediately to the bathroom and check her hairline, that was for damn sure. If she did, she'd be giving this story – this madness – a level of credibility that was undeserved.

"Hey Karen," Clare called as she came through the door, nodding at the college-aged girl who worked the counter.

"Ah, brilliant. You're early. Mind if I take off? I've got a huge exam tomorrow," Karen asked, pushing her glasses up her freckled nose.

"Go ahead, I've no problem with that. I come in late often enough as it is," Clare said, shooting Karen a breezy smile as she tucked her purse in a cubby and hung her coat on a hook.

"Oh, there's an envelope for you on the table. Some chap came by – one I wouldn't mind giving a good shag to, mind you – and left it for you. Said his name was Blake," Karen said as she swung out the front door, the chimes tinkling cheerfully after the info bomb she'd just dropped on Clare's head.

"I'm not going to read it," Clare said out loud to the shop. "I don't have to. I can keep my life exactly as it is."

She spent the next forty minutes dusting shelves and tidying the shop, her glance straying to the envelope on more than one occasion. After ringing up her third customer there was a momentary lull, and she settled in her chair by the table. Her eyes slid to the envelope.

"Damn it," Clare swore, and picked it up.

She'd known she was going to open it all along. It's funny the tricks we try to play on ourselves, isn't it? Clare slid her thumb beneath the edge of the envelope, peeling the flap open and pulling out the folded piece of paper. If she felt a thrum of power from the paper, she ignored it.

The silver-eyed ones will hurt you. Be vigilant. I can't protect you if you won't accept who you are.

Clare's hand shook as she dropped the paper to her lap and pressed the backs of her hands to her eyes. Had the last twenty-four hours really happened? Just yesterday morning, she'd been exploring a new avenue of research for her dissertation. Now she was seeing people with silver eyes, mysterious strangers were looking out for her, and a random grandmother knew her name and could read her mind.

Clare scrubbed her hands over her face again; then, taking a deep breath, she picked the letter back up and added the phone number found there into her phone. It wouldn't hurt to have it on hand, she thought. Staring around the store, Clare found herself being drawn to the pile of blue chalcedony, a stone that was used for protection. Slipping a piece into her pocket, she made a mental note to add it to her tab.

When the door chimed to announce a new shopper, Clare pasted a smile on her face and went to work. Unraveling mysteries were for another time.

Or if she would even get the time, Clare amended the thought as she slung her knapsack over her shoulder hours later and locked up. The shop had been impossibly busy that day – both a blessing and a curse, she supposed – and she hadn't had a moment to do any research at all. Neither for school nor on any of the nonsense that had been thrown her way in the last day or so.

Breathing out a sigh of relief that her day was over, Clare turned and let out a screech as she almost slammed into a mountain of black leather.

"Sorry 'bout that," Blake said, stepping back, his hands raised in apology.

Clare clasped a hand to her heart and worked to calm her breathing as she took in her instant response to his nearness. It was like her body had gone on full alert – even though he represented everything that scared her at the moment, her inner goddess rolled over and begged for him to come closer.

"You can't just creep up on women like that. It's not right," Clare said, her tone stiff.

"If I don't creep up on you, you'll slip away too easi-ly," Blake said, falling into step with her as she walked away from the store.

Clare angled her head, looking up at him through a curtain of her hair.

"That also sounds creepy, you know?"

Blake sighed and pressed his lips together before speaking.

"In normal circumstances, yes. But these aren't normal circumstances and you aren't a typical woman," Blake said as they rounded a corner onto a busier street. People rushed about here, students on their way to the pubs, others lugging grocery sacks on their way home to get dinner on. The wind and the wet hadn't let up all that much, but it was business as usual for Dubliners.

"Why, it sounds like you think you know me," Clare stated, tugging her cap onto her head to try to cut down on the amount of hair whipping around her face.

"I know more than you think, Clare MacBride of Clifden," Blake said, and a shiver went through Clare at his easy use of her name.

"Why are you stalking me?" she demanded, her hands gripped tightly around the straps of her knapsack. She wanted to kick something or someone, but instead just gritted her teeth as her mind raced to determine if she was in danger from Blake.

Aside from the danger of losing her mind in lust, that is.

Blake blew out an impatient breath and raked his hand through his dark hair.

"I'm not stalking you, I'm protecting you. We've discussed this already. Last night."

Clare stopped short, and Blake took a step or two more before he realized she was no longer beside him. When he turned to look at her, the golden hue of the streetlamp picked up the blue in his eyes and Clare felt his look sear her to the core.

"You killed someone last night. Because of me. You killed a man because of me." Clare spit the words out, the awful truth that she had deliberately pushed from her mind all day suddenly rising up, wanting to overtake her.

Blake cursed and, looking around, snagged Clare's arm and drew her to him, tucking her against him as he leaned against the wall. To anyone approaching, they'd look like lovers having a cuddle on the street.

Clare forced herself to breathe, his nearness suddenly putting her at an extreme disadvantage. Not only did she realize just how much he towered over her – both in height and width – but the close proximity seemed to fry the circuits in her brain a bit. A part of her desperately wanted to slip her hands inside his leather jacket and run her hands up his chest to see if the muscles hidden beneath his coat were everything she thought they might be.

Clare's mouth dropped open. What was wrong with her? She was a cool-headed scientist. Not one to be over-come by lust on a rainy night on the dark streets of Dublin.

"It wasn't a man," Blake said, his warm breath tickling her ear. Clare gulped as a low tug of lust slipped through her core.

"I'm sorry, say that again? You're telling me it wasn't a man, then?" Clare gasped, forcing from her mind the thoughts of taking a nip of Blake's bottom lip.

"Do most men dissolve in a silvery puddle when pierced with a dagger?" Blake asked.

"Well, um, no, they most certainly do not," Clare agreed, trying to look anywhere but up at his face. The wind picked up at her back and Blake tugged her closer, sheltering her from its assault.

"The Domnua," Blake said simply, and Clare finally looked up at him, confusion lacing her brain.

"The Domnu? Like the Goddess?"

"The Domnua, her children. The fae – and not the good ones. Like light to the dark, winter to spring, death to life – the Domnua are the silver-eyed ones. You can see them. Most can't."

"I... I... why can I see them?" Clare asked in confusion. She was still in the information-gathering mode of a scientist, although what her mind was trying to grasp now was the stuff of living fairytales.

"You're *Na Sirtheoir*. A Seeker."

Clare felt her hairline begin to burn again, and something in her stomach twisted and turned with recognition at the same word that Fiona had spoken to her earlier in the day.

"I don't know what that means. And I'm not looking to find out either," Clare said. She held up her hand when Blake opened his mouth. "You've got the wrong girl. I'm a scientist, not some sort of hunter. I just want to finish up my degree and get a job in the field I love."

"Scientist, you say. Isn't that a seeker of sorts? Seeker of knowledge? Seeker of truth? You hunt for answers?" A slight smile played across Blake's lips.

"Fine, you scored a point on that one. Kudos to you," Clare said sarcastically, pushing away from him. She stepped back, pausing as her eyes trailed over him – from his worn leather boots, up to his tight jeans, to the leather jacket that fit him like a second skin.

"You've got the wrong woman," Clare said again,

emphasizing each word so he would understand she meant what she was saying.

"I don't. But I'll keep protecting you until you figure it out," Blake said easily.

Clare brought her fists to her head, wanting to scream in frustration.

"I'm asking you to leave me alone," Clare said, speaking as though Blake was unable to understand complex thoughts.

"And I'm telling you that I'll be protecting you until you pull your head out of your arse and realize that there are bigger things on the line than whether you want to wrap your science-focused brain around the fact that there are fae – both good and bad fae, in fact – and the bad ones are trying to stop your breath on this lovely plane of exis-tence we're on. And until you force that gorgeous mind of yours to understand that you need to start working on your quest, you're pretty much sealing our doom."

Clare's mouth dropped open as her breath hitched. "Our doom?"

"Our doom. Mine, yours, and the fate of Ireland. Time is running out, Doc. What are you going to do about it?"

Clare shook her head at him, his words so outrageous – absurd, really – that she just could not compute what he was saying.

"I'm going home to curl up in my bed and think."

"Don't take too long, Doc. Time is slipping away."

Clare raced the rest of the way home, barely registering

the startled looks on people's faces as she darted past them.

Like the night before, Blake shadowed her the whole way home.

CHAPTER 8

*B*ianca was home when Clare burst into the apartment, feet tucked into cottage socks and propped on the living room table, a pile of books and a laptop computer next to her on the couch. Her pretty blue eyes widened in surprise at Clare's entrance.

"Day two of racing into the apartment like you're being chased. What's going on with you?"

Clare was careful to slide the deadbolt in place before dropping into the armchair, her coat still buttoned tight.

"I think I'm in trouble," Clare said, leveling a gaze at her roommate.

Bianca, to her credit, didn't even crack a smile. Instead, she straightened on the couch and picked up a pad of paper and a pen.

"Does it have something to do with *Na Sirtheoir*?"

Clare's mouth dropped open. "How did you know?"

"Duh, that's what I go to school for. You told me to

research it." Bianca spread her hands out to indicate the pile of books next to her.

"What have you learned?"

Bianca raised an eyebrow at her. "How much time do you have?"

Clare blew out a breath and reached up to tug the cap off her head. "Let me change into something more comfortable."

"I've got a lasagna in the oven. It seemed like just the night for it," Bianca called after her as Clare followed the narrow hallway down to her room.

"You're an angel, you are. A living, breathing angel," Clare called back before opening the door to her room.

Clare's bedroom was neat, and serviceable at best. A queen-sized bed was tucked next to a window with white linen curtains, a quilt in earth tones given to her by her mother lay across the bed, and a picture of her family was hung next to her favorite painting of the Cliffs of Moher. The only flight of whimsy in the room was a pretty crystal light-prism that Branna had given her, which Clare had hung so it would catch the light from the window.

Clare opened her narrow closet and carefully hung up and put away her work clothes, before pulling on fitted leggings and an oversized sweatshirt. Pulling her curls into a knot on top of her head, she left to rejoin Bianca.

"I've opened a red. I figured Italian food, red wine, you know." Bianca gestured to the glass she'd put on the table next to the sofa. Clare moved a few of the books and settled onto the couch next to Bianca, needing to be close to her friend right now.

Someone she could always trust.

Bianca slanted Clare a look over the rim of her wine glass.

"Do you want to tell me about your day or do you want me to go first?"

Clare considered it for a moment, but then decided that Bianca needed to have all the information. In short order, she detailed the full extent of her meeting with Blake the night before, leaving nothing out, all the way through the end of her day today – including Blake waiting for her at the shop. By the time she was finished, both women had downed their glasses of wine.

"It's proof of my undying love and devotion to you that I'm not calling you a nutter right now," Bianca pointed out, leaning over to snag the bottle of wine from the table in front of them, her blonde hair disheveled from her running her hands through it.

Clare regarded her silently as she added more wine to each of their glasses. Even though she knew Bianca could come across as flighty and dramatic, her friend had a sharp mind and she didn't make snap judgments.

"Now, since I've been being your friend now for going on eight years or so, I'm likely to be the first to tell you if you've gone off the rails. But you're not crazy. And you're dead serious in what you're telling me. Frankly, I'm surprised you're even entertaining any of this. It's so far outside of what you allow yourself to believe."

Interesting choice of words, Clare thought.

"Had I not seen a man dissolve into a silver puddle at my feet, I'd probably not be entertaining a single second of this."

"If you truly are *Na Sirtheoir*, you'll be marked," Bianca said matter-of-factly.

There it was again, the comment about being marked.

Clare shook her head, though the same spot on her head seemed to warm.

"You can't think I'm some mythological character who's been destined to do something, can you?" Clare laughed and took a sip of her wine. The smile dropped from her lips when she saw the serious look on Bianca's face.

"Well, I mean, yes, I can. Listen, it seems so irrational to you – a scientist – which I completely understand. But keep in mind that wound within great myths and legends lie these small kernels of truth. It's from those seeds of truth that stories blossom and grow, twisting and turning – a vine climbing up a wall – until the end result is quite often far from the truth and not quite believable. But buried deep within all the fantastical stories lies the tiniest seed of truth."

"How could I possibly be marked? And if I am – what does that mean?"

Bianca's face came alive with delight. "Well, my friend, settle in. It's story time."

Clare glanced at the bottle of wine, now almost empty. "Will I need more wine?"

"Oh, you'll for sure want another bottle. I have one breathing on the counter in the kitchen."

"I'll grab it. Then I'm settling in."

"Good, because it's time for you to learn a little more about your heritage."

Clare could only hope that her heritage didn't involve her being drawn into some mythological battle between humans and fae.

Because that certainly wasn't part of her life plan.

CHAPTER 9

"*A* long time ago, maybe 1600 years or so? Which, now that I think about it, needs to be exact because if the four cities, and four hundred years, and four women, four treasures, four months…" Bianca mulled, looking up into the air as she counted. Clare's eyes widened.

"Let's just keep going. I don't need an exact date," Clare said gently.

"Right, sorry. So, a famous Celtic creation myth has to do with when the Goddess Danu sent her children, along with four treasures from four great god cities, to the Island of Destiny to, well, fulfill their destiny."

"Inisfail. I've heard you tell this story. It's where Ireland's name comes from."

"Right, so the Goddess' kids are gifted with these great treasures because they needed some protection from those who already inhabited the island."

"There were people here?"

"Other gods, actually. Danu's sister's children."

"Oh, so like family," Clare nodded, taking another sip of her wine. The alcohol had dulled some of the nerves that bit at her stomach, and she was willing to be open-minded.

"Not the good kind of family. Like the black sheep of the family that you don't want to talk about or hang out with," Bianca amended.

Clare raised an eyebrow at her. "Go on."

"Where Danu was goodness and light, her sister, Domnu, was of the dark. They were polar opposites."

Clare felt herself grow cold and remembered Blake's words.

"Like winter to summer."

"Night to day," Bianca agreed.

"So the dark ones ruled the island," Clare said, shifting to tuck her feet beneath her.

"Domnu's children ruled. So, naturally, many a great battle was had. I mean, I could go on for hours here. This is where leprechauns spring from, the fae, people of the hills… it all comes from this great time of when Domnu's and Danu's children clashed."

"Talk to me about the fae," Clare said.

Bianca held up her hand. "It's all tied in. And I won't bore you – well, you know I don't think it's boring, but I'll keep this focused to the legends that concern you. Essentially, Danu's kids come, they bring these treasures, the treasures enhance their powers, and they drive Domnu's clan into the hills."

"The fae."

"Well, eventually people take over the land and they all become fae. So, you know, good fae and bad fae. But I'm getting ahead of myself." Bianca paused as the timer from the kitchen stove buzzed.

"I'll help. Keep talking," Clare said, standing and following Bianca into their tiny kitchen. The scent of garlic made her mouth water and her stomach growled in response.

Their galley kitchen held a tiny table with two chairs and a potted violet plant that Bianca somehow managed to keep alive. Painted a sky blue with white cabinets, it was a cheerful, albeit small, space. Used to maneuvering around each other in the tight space, they had dinner plated and were tucked away at their little table in a matter of moments.

"So, part of one of the great battles where Danu's children triumphed over Domnu's involved a major curse. Like big time magick type stuff."

Clare sliced into a corner of the square of lasagna on her plate, steam rising from the noodles, cheese bubbling out from the middle. She groaned and rolled her eyes at the first bite.

"I'm sorry to interrupt, but you've gone and outdone yourself. This is fantastic."

"Thank you! I've been working on this recipe. Tweaking it a bit. I think it's really starting to shine."

"I could eat the whole dish after the day I've had. Okay, go on, go on. I'll just be worshiping this meal over here while you tell the story."

Bianca chuckled, but her cheeks tinged with pink, telling Clare she was pleased with the compliment.

"In the great battle that ensues, a curse is laid upon the land. Well, a curse that *could* befall at some point if all the conditions are not met. Essentially, Domnu's children conceded defeat and disappeared into the hills. There was a promise of peace and that Danu's children would live safely upon the land – but only for sixteen hundred years. If, by the time the sixteen hundred years were up, Domnu's children had recovered the four treasures, then they would once again be allowed to rule the land."

Clare thought about it for a moment and then shrugged.

"I don't see what the big deal is – the treasures just need to stay locked up. What are the treasures anyway?"

"A stone, a spear, a sword, and a cauldron," Bianca recited.

"Those shouldn't be too hard to protect or keep hidden."

"Except, like all magickal things, it's virtually impossible to keep them safe. They're fluid and fickle, and mercurial, when deciding who their masters are. Within the first four hundred years or so, they slipped from sight. And so the *Na Sirtheoir* were anointed by Danu herself – as were the *Na Cosantoir*."

Clare tilted her head at that. "My Irish isn't that great. What does that mean?"

"The Protectors. The Seekers were anointed to find the treasures. The Protectors were anointed to protect those who sought. It's all very mystical and romantic, I think," Bianca said, sipping her wine and staring dreamily into the air for a moment.

Clare snapped her fingers and Bianca jumped.

"You're saying that essentially there's this band of people who are charged with finding these treasures before the time is up. And another group who protects them on their quest."

"Yes, but I'm not sure if I would precisely say people." Bianca bit her lip, a worried expression passing across her face.

"What's that supposed to mean?"

"I mean that the Seekers and the Protectors aren't entirely human. They've been given some... extra abilities, you know, to help on the quest."

Clare felt the tips of her ears begin to burn as energy started to hum in the pit of her stomach. Annoyed now, she pushed her wine glass away and studied Bianca.

"The long and the short of it is that these half-humans, or whatever, along with their fierce Protectors, have to find the treasures, or what... what happens?"

"The bad fae leave the hills and rule the land again."

"Oh, sure, brilliant. Just brilliant," Clare muttered, her mind desperately trying to disbelieve this story she was hearing.

But her heart was telling her differently.

"Yes, I mean, it's really quite dramatic. In the 1600th

year, the *Na Sirtheoir* are each given a chance for each of them to recover the treasure allotted to them. And all must be recovered in that timeframe, or the bad fae – the Domnua – win."

"The Domnua?"

"Yes. The, um, the children of Domnu. The silver-eyed ones. You know, like you saw the other night? That was a bad one. The Danula are the children of Danu, the good ones."

Clare blew out a breath and raked her hand through her hair, her hand crossing the spot on her hairline that seemed to itch incessantly.

"Okay, so, how come the *Na Sirtheoir* are only given four months apiece in the last year? Haven't they been seeking these treasures for ages?"

"It was one of the twists of the curse. Those who sought before the final year would only find clues – but never the treasures. It's all very mystical and confusing, as most legends and curses are."

"That's certainly a bitch, isn't it?"

"Yes, well. You know, ancient curses and all that. Can't make things too easy, now can they?" Bianca smiled at her.

"Listen, I'm not dumb. I think I know where you're heading with this. You're trying to say that I'm…" Clare trailed off as the reality of what she was about to say hit her. If she accepted this story as truth – and if she was involved – the world as she knew it was about to change. She held up her hand to shush Bianca.

"Have you ever had one of those moments in life? Those defining moments – like when you move across country or someone you love dies? It narrows life down into this sort of before and after tipping point. It becomes a marker in your life. Before I left for college, I was this person. Before so-and-so broke up with me, I was that person." Clare realized she was beginning to babble, and she looked helplessly across the table at Bianca. "Why do I feel like this is about to be one of those moments? You're trying to gently tell me that… that I'm…"

"You're one of the *Na Sirtheoir*."

CHAPTER 10

To her credit, Clare didn't faint or throw up. Instead, she stared dully at Bianca while the truth roared over her like a freight train.

"Hey, Clare, look at me. Clare," Bianca said sharply, snapping her fingers in Clare's face.

"Sorry, sorry, what?" Clare asked shaking her head as she narrowed in on Bianca's worried face.

"You've got to hold it together. If you're going to save the world and all," Bianca pointed out, and Clare felt that strange buzzing in her head start up again.

"I need to pause. Just pause for a damn moment while I try and take this all in," Clare said, taking a deep breath and trying to get centered.

"You just sit. I'm going to clear the table and get some tea going. I think we'll have a touch of the Irish too. Let's settle in and get this figured out."

Bianca bustled around the room, cleaning the plates,

putting a kettle on to heat, and pulling out Clare's favorite sleepy-time tea – chattering all the while about this and that, but never once bringing up the *Na Sirtheoir*.

Friends like that were worth their weight in gold, Clare thought. She tipped the name *Na Sirtheoir* around in her head, testing its weight, and found that its truth slipped through her like a cool river of knowledge.

Or like a key fitting into its lock.

Finally, Clare looked up at Bianca. "You can stop making small talk. I'm ready to accept this. To a point, I suppose. But I can't be denying the truth of it. At least way down in my gut." Clare clutched her hand in a fist at her stomach. "In this spot? I feel the truth of it. Sort of burning and humming and all this energy – right here. So, no, I can't be telling myself lies anymore."

Bianca breathed out a sigh of relief as she pulled the water from the stove and busied herself with getting the tea together.

"Sure and I'm glad to hear that. Because if that's the case – if you really, truly are *Na Sirtheoir*? We've a lot of work to do."

"*I* have a lot of work to do," Clare clarified, meeting her friend's eyes. "Not you. I'm not dragging you into this mess."

Bianca's hands came to her hips and her eyebrows rose almost to her hairline.

"Sure and you don't think I'll be sitting at home while you're off saving the world, now do you?" Bianca demanded, her voice rising. "I'm the trusty steed. The friend that helps you through the tough spots. Don't you know anything about how legends work? I'm the Sam to your Frodo. The Pippa to your Catherine, the Kit to your Vivian."

Clare struggled to keep up with her. "Wait, *Lord of the Rings* I get, but the Duchess and her sister? *Pretty Woman*? I don't know if those are all quests," Clare said, but she found her lips stretching into a smile, some of the weight of the moment lifting.

"The point is, I'm your person. The one that's going to be with you through this."

Clare smiled at her friend as she brought tea to the table. Looking up at Bianca, she raised an eyebrow in question. "But wouldn't that be this Protector person?"

"Who says you can't have more than one friend helping?"

And there you had it, Clare thought. The warrior doesn't win the battle on his own, does he? Why was she thinking she'd conquer this legend on her own?

"You can help. You can find the treasure for all I care. I'm still having a hard time absorbing this news."

"Why don't we check your mark? Then we'll know for sure if we've got to get started on finding the treasure – and if not? We'll go get a pint."

"I wouldn't even know where to start with finding a treasure," Clare pointed out as they both stood. "How would I even know which one to look for?"

Bianca looked at her in astonishment.

"Yours is the stone. Even I can see that."

"Well, that little clue was right in front of my eyes, wasn't it?" Clare said, feeling foolish. They made their way back into the living room and deposited their tea, along with a bottle of Middleton, on the table.

"You just aren't in clue-finding mode yet. You'll come along quickly," Bianca loyally assured Clare.

Clare rolled her eyes. "This could be a disaster. Either way – how do we find the mark?"

"Well, according to the book it's supposed to look like this," Bianca said, grabbing her laptop and clicking a few keys. She turned the screen and wordlessly held it out to Clare.

Clare blinked as she registered the symbol on the laptop. It was a play on the Celtic knot: four corners twisting into points, a circle connecting them all through the middle.

And she'd seen it just yesterday, when Branna had given her a necklace with the same symbol on it. Clare pulled it from where it was tucked beneath her shirt and held it up so Bianca could see it.

"No!" Bianca gushed, leaning forward to examine the pendant. "When did you get this?"

"Branna gave it to me yesterday. She said she'd thought I'd appreciate the symbol."

"Oh my goodness, Branna. It looks like we need to be having a little chat with her then, doesn't it?" Bianca asked.

"And with Fiona too. I think the old woman knows more than she let on."

"Plus, we can't forget Blake," Bianca pointed out as she pulled the laptop from Clare's hand and put it back on the couch.

"My head's already spinning," Clare admitted as she tried to piece together all the different avenues she would now have to pursue in her life. Assuming she was *Na Sirtheoir*, that is.

"Speaking of head, um, it says that the mark would be under the hairline," Bianca said.

Clare automatically pressed a hand to the spot at the nape of her neck that she so often found herself touching lately.

"Um, I'm assuming you know it's there, then?" Bianca tilted her head at Clare's gesture.

"I can't quite say. I've never looked. But if my day continues in the same vein that it has been going, well... I'm thinking it's right here." Clare turned and pointed to the spot.

"Let me look," Bianca said, coming to stand behind Clare. Her fingers were gentle as she parted Clare's hair, and Clare didn't need her to speak to know what she found. The quick hitch of Bianca's breath said everything.

"It's there, isn't it?" Clare asked quietly.

"It is. Let me snap a picture with my phone, hold on," Bianca said. Clare waited as Bianca grabbed her iPhone and snapped a picture. In moments they were on the couch together, peering at the phone's small screen.

"It almost looks like a tattoo," Bianca finally said.

"But I don't understand. I thought maybe, if anything,

it was a small mole. I've felt it sometimes, when I'm doing my hair. But a symbol? You'd think my hairdresser would have commented on it."

"Or your parents would have noticed it when you were a baby," Bianca pointed out.

"Oh, that's a good point, it is. What about when I was a baby?" Clare agreed, reaching over to grab her mug of tea. After a moment of consideration, she picked up the Middleton bottle and tipped a slug of the amber-colored liquid into her mug. If any occasion called for whiskey, it was this one.

"Maybe it just shows up when your time is near? Like your time for the mission?" Bianca asked, also pouring a generous amount of whiskey into her tea. She sipped it for a moment, studying Clare over the rim of her mug.

"Hmm, an invisible mark that only shows up when the legend is ready to be fulfilled. Sure, totally normal," Clare nodded.

"I think we zoomed past normal and turned a corner at fantastical about thirty minutes ago," Bianca said, making Clare snort and shake her head. Turning, she looked at her friend.

"Assuming this is real, and not some wild dream, what does it all mean? Where do I start? I don't even know why this stone is so valuable or what it looks like. Or what it's made of, for that matter. Am I supposed to just put my life on hold? Skip work, stop writing my dissertation, and just... go on a quest? That doesn't even make sense to me. It's so far away from anything I can even begin to comprehend. And you sit here nodding at me," Clare said help-lessly, taking a big gulp of her tea to stem the flow of words.

"Yes, I think that is what you've got to do. Stop every-thing and find this stone. Because – if this legend is true – life as we know it will end if the Domnua take over."

Clare snorted. "The Domnua. Fae. Fairytales. Fae taking over the world. It's all just so... farfetched."

"And yet weren't you the one that saw a silver-eyed man dissolve into a puddle on the street? Maybe not so farfetched after all."

Clare sighed and took another sip of her whiskey-laced tea, pulling her feet up under her legs on the couch.

"We need a plan."

"Oh, I've already started outlining stuff. Under the assumption you were *Na Sirtheoir*. So, we need to get you up to speed on the good fae and the bad fae, what their weaknesses and strengths are, how to identify them and so on. Then we have to look at the traits of the stone and try to track its history. Finally, I think we need to bring this Blake guy in and pick his brain. You said he seemed surprised that you knew nothing about him? That tells me he knows a lot more than he's letting on."

Bianca was jotting notes down on the pad of paper she held, her pen flying across the paper. Excitement laced her voice as she ticked off a list of things to do.

"Bianca, I don't know how you do this... I really don't. My head is spinning," Clare admitted.

Bianca reached out and patted her knee.

"I'm your R2D2."

"My… what?" Clare raised an eyebrow at her.

Bianca just laughed and bent her head back to the notepad.

"You'll figure it out."

CHAPTER 11

*C*lare hadn't wanted to sleep. Once she'd accepted – well, somewhat accepted – that she was *Na Sirtheoir*, she'd wanted to stay up and study all night. It was as though she were preparing for the biggest exam of her life and she didn't even know what was on the syllabus.

Bianca had finally bustled her off to bed, promising to make a Cliff's Notes version of what she needed to know. They'd decided that first thing in the morning they were going to pay a visit to Fiona. After that, they would track down Blake. From there they would split; Bianca would hit up some of the historical texts she had access to at Trinity College and Clare would stop at the crystal shop to talk to Branna.

All things said and done, by the time night rolled in, they should have a lot more information in their arsenal.

And from there – who knew?

Clare had managed a few hours' sleep, in between worry for the future of her schooling and worry for the future of Ireland. So, really, just the future in general, it seemed. Of everything. Ever. No big deal, right?

The evidence of a fitful night was made clear when Clare peered into the tiny mirror tucked above their bathroom sink. She groaned at the sight of the bags under her eyes.

"How long will you be?" Bianca called from the other side of the door.

"How long will it take to remove the bags from beneath my eyes?"

"Try my cucumber eye gel. And use the concealer in my makeup bag."

"Then fifteen minutes or so," Clare called, pulling off her towel and stepping under the lukewarm stream that piddled from their showerhead. One of the downsides of this apartment was crappy water pressure and a tiny kitchen. But the location was excellent and the price was right – so they'd compromised.

But on a morning like today? She'd be willing to give up naming rights to her first-born in exchange for a hot, steamy shower.

Clare made short work of the rest of her morning routine, marveled briefly at the cooling touch of the cucumber eye gel, and then breezed through a simple makeup application. Blessed with creamy skin, a smattering of freckles, and dark spiky lashes, Clare rarely added more makeup than a swipe of mascara or a hint of gloss. She gave a wave of her hand as she passed Bianca on the way back to her room.

She studied her outfit choices. A peek behind the curtain had revealed another gray day, so Clare pulled out her favorite dark skinny jeans, flat black boots that came to her knees, and a fitted black turtleneck sweater. She grabbed her black leather jacket from the hook on the back of her door and followed the scent of coffee to the kitchen.

Bianca took one glance at her and snorted.

"You look like you're going to rob someone. Or maybe go on a motorcycle ride."

Clare glanced down at her dark outfit and grinned.

"So maybe I am channeling my inner badass a bit. I mean, if I have to save the world – I'd better look the part, right?"

"That's the attitude! Here, read these over. I'll get some toast going," Bianca said, dropping a sheaf of notes on the counter. Clare grabbed them, along with a cup of coffee, and sat at their little table.

"Good fae vs. bad fae. The Danula vs. the Domnua. I'm going to have to remember these names," Clare muttered as she sipped her coffee. Black, like her outfit.

"It's more important that you remember how to iden-tify them and kill them than it is to remember what to call them," Bianca pointed out.

Clare put her cup down carefully and turned to stare at her roommate.

Today Bianca was dressed in a turquoise blue cardigan with a brilliant red lace top beneath. With her blonde hair in two braids and just a touch of makeup, she looked like a cheerful sixteen-year-old ready to go shopping with her friends.

Not someone who would calmly discuss killing fae over toast and coffee.

"What? Why are you looking at me like that? Don't you want to know how to kill them if they're coming after you?"

"I suppose that's wise," Clare agreed and skimmed the notes written in Bianca's sharp, neat handwriting.

"Silver eyes and a silver glow. That's bad," Clare said, looking up at Bianca.

"Yup, or anyone dressed completely in silver. Fae are drawn to shiny things so anyone over the top covered in silver, that kind of thing. Pretty much just look for the glowing silver eyes and you should know."

"Will you be able to see them?" Clare asked, suddenly curious about how that worked.

Bianca shook her head, a sad expression on her face.

"No, much to my despair. It seems that's part of your gift. You'll be able to pick them out of the crowd pretty easily. Otherwise they just look like normal humans to regular people like myself."

"How come I haven't seen them before now?"

"The clock started ticking for you about two weeks ago, that's why. They're beginning to circle."

Nerves skittered through Clare's stomach and she swallowed against her suddenly dry throat.

"Bianca, you should go home for a while. Just... just

until this is over. I can't put you in danger," Clare ordered, steel lacing her voice.

"Sorry, no can do. I'm the Bonnie to your Clyde," Bianca said cheerfully.

"Why am I Clyde?" Clare demanded.

"Because your name begins with a C. Duh," Bianca said, as she settled across from Clare. "Now, pay attention. Bad fae will be silver everything. Good fae are going to be violet. Violet eyes, violet hue, violet clothes. Something to do with royalty or auras, not entirely sure on that one."

"Will the purple ones help me?"

"I believe so. Though I would approach with caution. Carrying your weapons, of course."

"And what weapons would these be?" Clare asked, spreading orange marmalade across her toast as she studied Bianca.

"Well, iron for one. Fae hate iron. That's pretty much a given."

"Is it? Well, I must have missed that along my studies," Clare said dryly.

Bianca chuckled. "Iron, whatever the stone itself is made of, ice, and emeralds," she continued matter-of-factly.

"Wait, ice?"

"Yup. It seems you can freeze them to death. Fae hate the cold."

"Don't we all?" Clare murmured, taking another sip of her coffee and feeling the caffeine begin to kick its way through her system.

"The emerald thing got me, though. I mean, emeralds? Isn't this the Emerald Isle? You'd think they'd gain great power from emeralds, not the other way around."

"You know, I do have a little emerald ring my grandmother gave to me," Clare mused.

Bianca pointed a finger at her across the table. "Put it on. And we are going to the store before we go see this Fiona lady. Time to arm ourselves with some iron."

"Aye, aye, Captain. Let's get started."

ON THE WAY to the store, Clare called the pub and told them she was quitting. The university would be another story – but since she didn't teach again until next week, she figured she had a little time to figure it out. And since she'd be seeing Branna in person later in the day, they could hash out the details of Clare leaving the shop then. Clare wondered just how much Branna knew about this legend. She was a great admirer of stones, after all; plus she'd given Clare that necklace. Odds were high that Branna had solid information.

The man at the hardware store gave them an odd look as they both loaded their backpacks with a variety of iron tools – small garden shovels, nails, a few chains, and a couple of hand-held stakes.

"You girls working on building something?" The man leaned back and crossed his arms over his chest.

"We're in a play in college," Clare said smoothly.

The man nodded. "Must be a gardening scene."

"Yes, watching flowers grow is spell-binding," Bianca quipped. They giggled the whole way out of the store while the man just shook his head after them.

"Here, put some nails in your pocket too. It's probably good to have them easily accessible," Bianca instructed. Soon Clare had pieces of iron tucked all over her body.

"I'm covered. Sure and it feels weird. I feel like I should be scanning constantly now – trying to find fae."

"Do you think they come out during the day?" Bianca wondered.

"You can't think I'd be knowing the answer to that!" Clare exclaimed as they pushed past a tourist group wandering the street in front of Christchurch Cathedral, the tour guide droning about the history of the church.

"Fine, next question. Should we have rung up this Fiona character first?"

"I get the impression she'll be expecting us. She's got power, by the way."

Bianca squealed and clutched Clare's arm in delight. "Two people with power! Oh, this is so exciting," Bianca declared, winking at a cute guy who smiled back at them as he passed.

"You still haven't told me what my power is, besides seeing fae," Clare said as they stopped in front of a hotel tucked around the corner from the fashionable gallery district.

"Swanky place," Bianca murmured while they pushed inside.

"Are you dodging the question?" Clare asked.

"No, I'm just figuring you'll be wanting to talk about it when a bunch of people aren't listening," Bianca said, a bright smile on her face for someone over her shoulder.

Clare turned to find a man with a trim beard and a tailored suit smiling at them over the long counter that ranged along one side of the lobby, which was done up in sleek white with neon green and grey accents.

"Can I be helping you ladies today?"

"We're looking for Fiona..." Clare blanked out. She knew Fiona had given her last name, but now for the life of her, she couldn't remember what it was.

"Clare MacBride?" the man asked, an easy smile on his face.

"Yes, that's me," Clare said, shooting a glance at Bianca.

"You're to head up to the penthouse. Fiona has breakfast set out for you. Please let me know if there's anything else we can see to while you're here."

Clare nodded in response and turned toward the elevator, her mind churning. The penthouse? The woman hadn't struck her as being particularly rich.

Bianca stayed quiet until they were in the elevator, then let out another high-pitched squeal.

"The penthouse! I've always wanted to see inside a penthouse. And at this fancy hotel too? I'm dying," Bianca gushed, fanning her face.

"Just keep the iron in your hand. We have no idea what we're walking into," Clare said, pulling a small stake from her pocket.

Bianca sobered instantly. "You're absolutely right about that one. I need to keep my game face on, that's for damn sure."

The elevator doors slid open silently to a small corridor that led to a single door. Before they'd even had a chance to knock, the door swung open.

"Clare, Bianca, you're welcome here."

CHAPTER 12

*F*iona looked like everyone's favorite grandmother, but amped up a bit. With hair longer than most women her age, and a brisk white shirt tucked into slim khaki pants, she had a worldly sort of air about her. Clare couldn't help but admire the twisted necklace of amethyst and quartz wound around her neck.

Clare's hand tightened on the stake.

Fiona glanced down at Clare's hand and then met her eyes.

"As I said, you're welcome here. You're also safe here. Safer than you'd be out on the streets. You have no reason to fear me."

"Said every bad guy in a movie ever," Bianca quipped; Fiona chuckled, the sound tinkling like a bubbling brook.

"I'm here to help. I have no stake in this game other than fulfilling a promise to a ghost and making sure that Ireland stays safe."

"A ghost," Bianca gasped, her eyes shining with interest. "Tell me everything."

"Come along then, I've got a table set up for us."

Clare followed them reluctantly, her eyes darting around the penthouse. The same theme of white, gray, and green was echoed here, but in a much more subdued manner. Soft grey carpet covered the floors, and white couches with fat green pillows sat at angles in a sitting room. Clare caught a glance of a pristine white king-sized bed through the bedroom door.

They turned down a small hallway that led to a larger room with a full dining room table and floor-to-ceiling windows that looked out over a large patio area as well as the entire city of Dublin. A spotless white linen tablecloth covered the long dining table. Bright green napkins sat folded on top of plates, and silver serving trays sat on a sideboard next to the table.

"What a view!" Bianca exclaimed.

"Yes, well, I've lived simply for much of my life. I figured it was time to splurge, now that John is back with me," Fiona said simply and gestured for them to sit. Clare wondered just where John had been, considering Fiona had introduced him yesterday as the love of her life.

"Tea?" Fiona asked and they nodded.

"Fiona, can you tell me more about yourself? How you came to find me? Why are you involved in this?" Clare asked, and Bianca shot her a glare. "What? I'm just trying to get answers."

"It's fine, we can dispel with niceties when there are

more important things at stake," Fiona said gently. "Why don't you fill your plates? I've ordered way too much food, and there's a bit of everything, really."

Clare didn't have to be told twice. Her metabolism usually kicked along at a pretty high pace; so far she had been blessed with being able to eat what she wanted. The downside was that she got quite cranky if she hadn't eaten for several hours.

In a matter of moments, they were all sitting at the pretty table, their plates piled high with rashers of bacon, steaming mounds of fluffy scrambled eggs, and two different types of scones.

"Please, go ahead and eat. I suppose it's best that I talk for a bit."

Clare nodded, biting back the snarky comment that threatened. Of course this woman had some explaining to do. She came out of nowhere and expected Clare to believe her nonsense tales? Yeah, she'd better start talking.

"I live out in the hills by a small fishing village called Grace's Cove," Fiona began.

Clare nodded. "South of where I grew up," she said.

"Correct. It's a lovely spot and home to my family and my work."

"What is it you do?" Bianca asked politely as she smothered her scone in butter.

"I'm a healer," Fiona said with a smile.

"Like a nurse?" Bianca asked.

Clare sat back and studied Fiona.

"No, she means in the old ways. With her hands."

"Ohhhh," Bianca breathed, then shoved a scone in her mouth, probably to cut off the flow of questions she wanted to ask.

Fiona chuckled and tucked a silver strand of hair behind her ear. Pretty turquoise drops set in silver sparkled there.

"You've more power than that, though," Clare commented, her eyes on Fiona.

"Aye, I've more power than that. My strongest is my healing. But through the years I've learned to develop many of my other strengths. Some mind-reading, some spell-casting, some empath powers, the likes of those," Fiona explained.

"So what am I thinking right now?" Bianca demanded.

Fiona eyed the blonde for a moment before a smile broke out on her face.

"That you want to break up a scone to feed the pigeons on the patio," Fiona said.

Bianca's mouth dropped open in excitement. Turning, she grabbed Clare's arm. "Did you hear that? She read my damn mind. I'm so impressed. I wonder what else she can do," Bianca exclaimed and then a blush swept her cheeks immediately after. "I'm sorry. I'm sorry. That's entirely too rude of me. You aren't a circus act to perform on demand."

"No, I'm most certainly not. You'll have to take my word for it, I suppose," Fiona said, but there was no sting behind her words.

"So you live in the village, you use your magick regularly, and then... what? Something prompted you to come find me. What was that exactly?" Clare asked as she picked up a crispy slice of bacon.

"Let's just say… there was a major gift given to me. A boon, so to speak. And in return, I was tasked with finding you and assisting you on your quest," Fiona said carefully.

"Dark magick?" Clare asked.

"No, no, nothing of the sort. Familial magick. I told you I was descended from the great Grace O'Malley – and you're a branch of that family too. We're blood. And it was one of Grace O'Malley's own who insisted I come to help you on your path. So, here I am."

"This was the ghost?" Bianca breathed, the scone in her hand forgotten halfway to her mouth.

"This was the ghost," Fiona agreed, flashing her a quick smile.

"I swear, I think I'd just die if I saw a ghost in person," Bianca said, and shuddered dramatically.

"Oh, but you're fine with hunting and killing fae?" Clare asked Bianca.

"Well, yeah. I mean, aren't fae real – like a real threat? Ghosts aren't really a threat to you."

"Actually, my dear, ghosts are real and can be a threat, but they also can be good. But since you've brought up fae, we might as well get into the details of the task at hand."

Clare wanted to snort at the word "task." Task implied running to the corner store for more milk. A task was finishing the citations in her dissertation. Hunting down an ages-lost treasure while also fending off evil fae was not something she would refer to as a task.

"We've done a little homework since I saw you yester-day," Clare said, reaching for a squat white pot in the middle of the table to add some cream to her tea.

"Ah, I see. Go on," Fiona gestured with her teacup.

"We believe I'm *Na Sirtheoir*. You were right."

A smile crossed Fiona's face – the pleased smile of the teacher who has been surprised by the student.

"You are. But I'm glad you discovered that on your own. Much more difficult for a stranger to point it out to you. As told by the way you ran from the coffee shop."

"And, because my roommate is a stellar researcher, she has discovered there are also Protectors. As well as that my little task must be accomplished in four months, and that the treasure I am to find is some magickal stone."

Fiona smiled again. "That neatly sums it up, though you've left out the bit about the fae."

"Right, and fae are trying to kill me," Clare said bitterly.

"*Some* fae are trying to kill you," Bianca amended quickly.

Fiona beamed at her. "You're much further along than I anticipated. Why don't you start with questions? It seems you've covered a lot of ground already."

"What's so great about this stone?" Clare asked.

"Ah, yes, I suppose you should know what you're fighting for, shouldn't you?" Fiona leaned back in her chair and crossed her arms over her chest, her eyes going a bit dreamy as she considered her words.

"It was a treasure brought from the great city of Falias. It's often referred to as the Stone of Destiny," Fiona began.

Bianca gasped. "The singing stone!"

"Yes, well, not so much anymore. There's more than one these days," Fiona chuckled.

"But originally it sang?" Clare looked around in confusion.

"When the rightful ruler held this stone, it would sing. It was used to determine the next worthy ruler of the realm," Fiona said.

Clare worked that little nugget of information around in her head as she thought about the power she often felt from stones.

"But you say it doesn't do that anymore?" Bianca asked.

"With any magickal thing, its essence often grows and changes. The stone, lost now for twelve hundred years or so, has passed through many hands – both fae and human. It's gained its energy from these new sources and has adapted. Magick is tricky, and the stone is mercurial. I've heard one of its greatest powers is that it allows the holder to discern truth."

Bianca and Clare both paused at that, their eyes meeting across the table.

"Like a lie detector?"

"Very much so. But you don't need to be actually quizzing the subject to know if they are lying. So long as the stone sits with you, you can read anyone's intentions at any time. To put that in perspective, consider the leader of a nation holding that stone."

Both Bianca and Clare sat in stunned silence.

"A leader can hold the stone and ask if North Korea plans to drop a bomb, and the stone will reveal what is truth and what is lies. They don't even have to be in the same room with the subject."

"That's... that's..." Bianca sputtered.

"Insanity. Entirely way too much power for one person to hold," Clare finished for Bianca.

"Precisely." Fiona nodded at them in agreement.

"What makes you think I won't run off with this stone and rule the world? I mean, I am human. We have weaknesses." Clare studied Fiona over the rim of her cup.

"You're *Na Sirtheoir*. It is your destiny to find and protect the stone. Thus it won't have an overpowering effect upon you," Fiona said.

"In other words, don't let me get to it first," Bianca teased, but Fiona turned a careful gaze upon her.

"Unfortunately, that's entirely correct. You shouldn't let any human touch the stone once you have it."

"But where am I going to deliver this stone? How am I going to store it? Is it big?" The questions just tumbled out of Clare's mouth. So much to learn, and they were already racing against the clock.

"I'm not sure the size of it, to be quite honest. I was only given so much information." Fiona spread her hands in apology. "But I do know that you will be given help along the way. You've only to ask for it."

"Like, um, 'hey gods and goddesses – show me where the stone is'?" Clare asked.

A wide smile flashed across Fiona's face, showing her beauty.

"It's certainly worth a shot. But I suspect it won't be so easy. You know about the fae, then?"

"I saw one killed the other night," Clare admitted, focusing on buttering her scone and not the image of the fae dissolving into a puddle on the ground.

"A Domnua, I hope?" Fiona asked.

"Yes, a silver one."

"Ah, very well then. Sure and you didn't kill him yourself? Who did?"

"It seems my Protector has arrived," Clare said bitterly.

"And he's hot, too. Or so I'm picturing," Bianca gushed, earning a glare from Clare.

"Ah. Isn't that interesting," Fiona mused, pursing her lips as she looked out over the Dublin skyline where the grey clouds still held the city hostage.

"In what way?" Clare demanded.

"That you find him attractive so far as I can tell. And that he's shown himself already. I suspect that means you've already been in danger more than you've realized. *Na Cosantoir* don't like to be seen, from what I gather. It seems they prefer to keep a low profile; often the *Na Sirtheoir* don't even realize they're being protected."

"But I've seen him twice now," Clare argued.

"Then you were meant to see him," Fiona said.

"Can you tell us more about the Danula? The good ones? How can we get them to help us?" Bianca asked, her eyes wandering to the sideboard where the platters of food lay.

"Get more bacon," Clare said with a sigh, knowing her roomie's love for bacon.

"Is that okay?" Bianca asked, and Fiona chuckled.

"Eat all you like; it's here for you."

"Brilliant," Bianca muttered. She stood and then waved a hand. "Continue, please."

"One thing I am allowed to tell you – the Danula must help you if you ask them. I'm asking that you be remembering that particular rule. It could save your life."

Clare swallowed at the enormity of the weight that suddenly pressed down on her shoulders.

"But… what about my life? As in – how it is now? My jobs? Our apartment? My schooling? Do I just… say goodbye? Go on some insane treasure hunt never to return – or to return and find the life I left in shambles?"

"Did you ever consider that maybe your life needs to be shaken up?"

At those words, a spark of anger worked its way through Clare. Tilting her chin up, she eyed Fiona.

"No, I haven't considered it. I've worked damn hard to get where I am and I'm very proud of myself."

"As you should be, child. I'm merely saying that things have a way of working themselves out. Remember, you can ask for help. With anything. Think about it when you come to any crossroads."

It wasn't until they were back outside, with Fiona's contact information in their phones and a fat envelope in Clare's hand, that Clare really understood what Fiona meant.

"She thinks we should just go for it and the rest will fall into place. If we ask for it to be okay – it will be okay," Clare said.

"So don't worry about rent and jobs and it will all work itself out?"

Clare flipped up the flap of the envelope to reveal a pile of cash with a note on top that read *rent money*.

"I think we just got our first gesture of help."

CHAPTER 13

"*W*ell, now that the rent is taken care of – what's next on the list? Finding Mr. Tall, Dark, and Mysterious? Is there like a bat signal you can shine?" Bianca asked as they strolled through the Temple Bar area, digesting what they had learned that morning. Clare, now that she'd been debriefed on what her new reality would be, was scanning the crowds of tourists to see if she could spot any otherworldly creatures.

"Nope, but I suspect I have an even better way," Clare murmured. A teenager dressed in a khaki coat with a hat tugged low on his head leaned nonchalantly against a building. His eyes met hers for a millisecond before sliding away.

"Hey!" Clare shouted across the street and Bianca jumped, clutching her arm.

The teenager didn't acknowledge them. Instead he

turned away and began walking, his steps hurried, but strikingly smooth.

"Hey! You! Come here!" Clare shouted after him and the kid picked up speed, never once glancing back. In less than a second, he'd zipped around the corner and disappeared.

"Holy… What the hell? Did you see how fast he moved? It was like he was gliding across the ground!" Bianca exclaimed, her mouth hanging open.

"His eyes were silver," Clare said, her gaze fixed on the spot where the teen had disappeared.

"And you thought it was best to call him out? What are you doing? Trying to get us killed?" Bianca gasped.

"Your friend raises an excellent question."

Clare stiffened at the voice behind her, but the timbre of it seemed to wind its way warmly around her stomach. Bracing herself for impact, she turned and met Blake's eyes head on.

"Oh, well, yes, I see now," Bianca said, her voice carrying a note of awe. "You must be Blake."

"I am. Nice to meet you, Bianca," Blake said, but his eyes never left Clare's face. He seemed to be searching her face for answers, answers she wouldn't – or couldn't – give. His dark hair was subdued by a grey knit hat, and he was in his customary dark jeans and zipped-up black leather jacket. Clare didn't want to think about how the daylight highlighted the blue of his eyes, deepening the color to an almost ocean blue.

Nope, she didn't want to think about that at all.

"Nice to meet you too," Bianca said automatically, then leaned in and whispered to Clare, "He's dreamy."

Blake's eyebrow rose but he didn't say anything.

"At least I know how to get you to show yourself if I need you," Clare said, breaking the silence that stretched between them, along with the hum of something else – something visceral and not altogether unpleasant.

"Oh, is that why you were yelling at that kid? You knew Blake would show up!" Bianca exclaimed, nodding. "Smart move."

"Not a smart move at all. Now, instead of eliminating the Domnua, you've called attention to your location and informed them that you're aware of them. In other words, you've blown your cover. In more ways than one."

Clare flinched at his words, hating the truth she found in them.

"I didn't quite think that one through now, did I? Listen, I'm only about a day into all this. I haven't had a chance to strategize. I'm still absorbing and learning. So cut me some slack," Clare said, glaring at Blake.

"If I cut you slack, you're dead," Blake said evenly, and Clare flinched again.

"Maybe if you'd have given me more background, I wouldn't be stuck trying to figure half of this out on my own," Clare countered, all but whining.

"We need to get moving. Now," Blake said as he grabbed Clare's arm and began dragging her forcibly down the street. Bianca hurried to catch up to them.

"Hey! You can't manhandle her like that. I'll stake the back of your neck," Bianca threatened from behind them.

Blake didn't even glance back as he kept propelling Clare down the street. With a swift turn, he led them down a more deserted side alley. Rounding on Clare, he let go of her arm and went nose-to-nose to her.

Well, almost nose-to-nose. Since he was easily a foot taller, it was more like chin-to-forehead. Clare's mouth went dry as her eyes traveled his leather-clad chest all the way up to his mutinous face.

"You will not pull something like that again. Do you understand me? It isn't just about what you want or need in that moment. Wanting to see me doesn't mean you get to jeopardize all of Ireland's future. This is not the time to be petty or selfish," Blake lectured her.

Clare felt her shoulders hunch and she shoved her hands deep into the pockets of her coat.

"I'm sorry, I wasn't thinking."

"See? She said she's sorry. Enough with the big tough guy act," Bianca ordered from next to Clare.

"No, he's right, Bianca. 'Twas foolish of me to pull a stunt like that. I should've remembered that I had his phone number. I'm not used to thinking for the greater good. He's right to be mad at me. I could have ruined the entire quest less than a day in."

Blake reached in his pocket and pulled out a small black flip phone and handed it to Clare.

"Now that things are… escalating, it's best if you don't

use your phone much. If you want to reach me, call me on this. It's protected."

"I haven't seen a flip phone in ages," Bianca said, looking down at the small phone in Clare's hand.

"That's the point. It can't be hacked by clever fairies."

"Oh, sure, right," Bianca said, nodding her head knowingly.

Clare sighed and looked up at Blake again. The wind was beginning to pick up and the first drop of rain hit her cheek.

"Can we talk to you somewhere private? We have a lot of questions."

Blake looked around and then back down at Clare.

"Meet me in an hour at O'Doole's Chemist. The back door. By Trinity."

And with that, Blake vanished. Before them one moment and, in a blur of movement, gone the next.

Bianca slapped a hand to her heart and sucked in a breath.

"I don't know if I'll be getting used to the quick-exit stuff these magick people can pull."

Clare glanced down the now-empty alley, the hairs on the back of her neck rising.

"Come on. I don't feel good about being here. Let's go talk to Branna and then meet his majesty at the chemist."

"Ohhh, I like that. He really is quite dreamy. I think you've picked a good one there."

Clare rolled her eyes as Bianca pattered on about

Blake's dreaminess, but kept her wits about her as she scanned for fae. It was the dawn of a new type of life for her – and she'd do well to remember what she was up against.

CHAPTER 14

*B*lake turned the corner, his dagger out, and sliced through the heart of a fae who had been eavesdropping on their conversation. The teenager melted to a puddle at his feet, and Blake kept moving, his dagger slicing through the next one coming fast.

Wiping the silvery blood from the dagger onto his dark jeans, he sheathed the knife and stormed through the city streets, people automatically making way for this tall man who vibrated with anger.

Of all the stupid things she could have done, Blake thought and cursed again, to call upon a Domnua had to be right at the top.

Had the fae not seen Blake over her shoulder, she'd have had a fight on her hands.

Blake had wanted to shake Clare, or in the alternative, throw her over his shoulder and take her back to his lair so he could keep watch on her at all times.

The roomie was an unexpected complication in that plan. But he couldn't deny that he liked her, and Clare too.

Though his liking for Clare seemed to be bordering more on red-blooded lust. Something he would do well to keep in check so as not to compromise the mission at hand.

Blake reached the chemist shop and went around back, pausing at the back door to key in his code. He felt the brush of his magickal wards as he stepped onto his protected area and into the back entranceway.

"Boss?"

"Aye," Blake called, stepping into the chemist shop instead of heading down into his workroom.

"Find her?"

"Stupid girl called out a Domnua. In the middle of broad daylight in the Temple Bar district," Blake said as he stepped into the shop. While the streetside windows housed a row of medicine bottles and lotions, it was just a facade. The actual room held four tables, all with various computers and lab equipment set up on them. His assistant sat at one of them.

"That's un-fecking-believable. Even for her," Seamus turned and shook his head in surprise.

"I swear to you, I almost strangled her on the spot."

"I can't quite blame you," Seamus agreed, and then cleared his throat. "Er, was Bianca with her by chance?"

"The bubbly blonde one with a few extra curves? Aye, she was there."

"Brilliant. Now Clare's leading her into the line of

fire," Seamus muttered, running a hand through his hair so that it tufted up in all directions.

"They'll be here in an hour's time. You'll have plenty of time to yell at them then."

"What!" Seamus screeched and pushed back from the computer he was working at. "You'll be blowing my cover then."

"It's past time to blow it. Clare's not going back to school. She's on the mission now. We might as well all work together."

Seamus pressed his lips together and paced the room, his face twisted in concern.

"I don't know if I want Bianca to know what I am," Seamus finally admitted.

"Seems to me she's pretty jazzed up about everything fae. I don't see her having much problem with you," Blake pointed out as he unzipped his jacket and hung it over a chair.

"You think?" Seamus's face brightened.

Blake cursed. "Yes, I think. Now we're moments away from reciting poetry when we should be planning how to find this treasure."

"There's always time for matters of the heart, my friend, always time for matters of the heart," Seamus sang as he moved back to his computer station.

Blake just shook his head and opened his laptop, and began to make a list.

And wondered just what the ladies would think when they found out that Seamus was a Danula.

CHAPTER 15

*C*lare paused in mid-stride as she opened the door to the crystal shop, her eyes taking in the slight shimmer of violet that tinged the edges of Branna's body.

"I'll be damned," Clare said.

Branna looked up from where she was helping a customer choose a piece of quartz.

"Clare, Bianca, always lovely to have the both of you in for a visit. Why don't you pop in the back and get the kettle heated?" Branna asked easily, and returned to helping the customer. Clare narrowed her eyes at Branna's back, but continued past the main room and through the beaded curtain that separated the front shopping area from the back employee lounge and stock room.

"What are you damned about?" Bianca commented as she settled into a worn mustard-colored couch covered in fat white peony blossoms.

"She's Danula."

"Ohhhh. Shut up! Oh, man, I'm so jealous. How come you get to see all the fun stuff and I don't? I'm the one who should be seeing this stuff. I went to school for it, didn't I?" Bianca demanded as Clare filled the electric tea kettle and switched it on. Turning, she leaned back against the counter and crossed her arms over her chest.

"I didn't see any of this stuff prior to yesterday, I'd just like to point out," Clare said.

"Maybe you did, but you didn't know that you could, and now that you know, you can," Bianca said.

Clare tilted her head as she followed Bianca's train of thought as it bounced around. "Perhaps," she finally agreed.

The chimes on the front door tinkled as the customer left, and a moment later Branna swept through the beaded curtain.

"I couldn't tell you," she said immediately.

"I can't believe it. I just can't believe you wouldn't tell me!" Clare exclaimed, anger washing through her. She'd always considered Branna to be practically a second mother, and had looked up to the older woman since the day they'd first started working together.

"It's part of the rules. I couldn't say anything. Nobody could. Until you saw your first fae on your own, we couldn't reach out to you or the quest would be destroyed."

"How does that even make sense? That has to be the stupidest clause I've ever heard," Clare bit out, turning as the kettle clicked off. She automatically pulled out three mugs from the cupboard and poured the hot water into the cups. Dropping teabags in each, she moved across the room and sat next to Bianca on the couch. Branna settled in a leather armchair across from them. Now that Clare could see the violet glow, it seemed that Branna positively shone and shimmered as she talked.

"Is that why you opened a crystal shop? You know, 'cause you like shiny things?" Bianca asked, pointing to the bangles and bracelets that lined Branna's arms almost to her elbows. Bianca had a point; Branna was always covered in scads of jewelry.

"Partly, yes. Plus I'm a crystal fae, so I can harness and draw upon their energies," Branna said simply, picking up her mug and blowing on the water.

Bianca's mouth dropped open in surprise. Clare knew she probably had a million more questions, but she held up her hand to stop Bianca from speaking.

"I'm really upset with you," Clare said quietly.

"I swear on my life, my shop, and our friendship – I would have told you if I could have." Branna's eyes – now a gray-violet color – met Clare's.

"Think about it, Clare. What if the fae had been bothering you when you were a kid? If you'd seen the silver-eyed ones then, man, could you imagine? They'd have said you were a nutter. It was probably to protect you," Bianca said, rocking forward in her seat with the earnestness of her words.

Branna smiled at Bianca.

"She's right. And some of this just has to wait until the time is right. I've been waiting since the new year dawned, doing my best to keep track of you, see if you'd learned anything yet. I had hoped to be the first to reach you once we were allowed to speak. Who was?"

"My Protector. A Domnua tried to attack me in a dark alley on my walk home from work the other night."

"*Na Cosantoir*? Ah, well, that's a relief. I was wondering when he would show up."

"How do you know it's a he?" Clare asked.

"Though it may seem misogynistic to you in this day and age, years ago it was meant to be a good thing that men were the Protectors," Branna said gently.

"Plus they let you do the hunting, so, you know, it isn't totally sexist. It's kind of a big deal to be the one who seeks the treasure, right?" Bianca asked.

"It is. An honor in its own right. Though it may not feel like one," Branna conceded.

"I can ask you for help then? You're bound to help me?" Clare asked, finally leaning over and picking up her mug of tea.

"I'd help you either way, as you're dear to me," Branna said with a soft smile.

Clare felt the warmth of Branna's love pulse through her and she knew the words to be true. Sighing, she leaned back in her chair.

"We have to leave to go meet Blake shortly. And I don't know where that is going to take us. Or when we'll be back. And I'm worried about my job here. I'm worried for you too. Hell, I'm just worried." Clare bit down on her lip as the enormity of her situation seemed to crash down around her. Surprised to find tears spike her eyes, she pressed the backs of her hands to her face.

"Oh, let me get you a tissue," Bianca said immediately, but Clare waved her to sit.

"I'm scared. I'm scared for you, for my family, for Ireland. In a matter of hours, my life has been flipped upside down and – what if I fail? What if I let everyone down?"

And that was the root of it really – if she failed, the fae would break the seal and Ireland and the world would be overrun by the Domnua. It was a heavy burden and not one she was sure she was equipped to carry.

"Well, first of all, your job will still be here. Your dissertation will hold; they will happily give you an extension. You can get a job at another pub whenever you feel like it. So, on that end, you'll be more than fine. As for the rest of it, I can't stress enough that you are not alone on this path. Nobody ever really is, you know. You've but to ask for help." Branna's eyes held hers.

"But I can't ask you where the stone is."

"Trust me, if we knew, we'd have taken it ages ago," Branna said.

"And, well, can I say something – about the failure thing?" Bianca raised her hand timidly and Clare nodded at her.

"It's just that… with anything in life, you take risks. You take a risk when you step outside your door that a car is going to run you over in the street. Or even if you don't leave your house – you can slip in the shower and hit your head and bleed out."

Clare's eyes widened at that, but Bianca was on a roll.

"And if you stay so scared, caught in your little corner or bubble, that you never take a risk – only because you're afraid of failure – well, in essence you've already failed. You've become the exact embodiment of the fear you are trying to avoid. So, you know, I don't think you *can* fail. Even if you don't find the stone. The only way you really will fail is if you go back to hiding in the lab on campus and trying to finish your dissertation." Bianca blinked and looked around at the women who stared at her.

"You've a wise friend along with you on your quest," Branna finally said.

"She's one in a million, that's for sure," Clare agreed. She stood, stretching her arms briefly above her head before looking down at Branna.

"You've a question for me?" Branna asked, reading it in her eyes.

"If you can't tell me where it is, can you give me a clue? A direction to start in? Something to go on?"

"Aye, I can," Branna rose and went to her desk, tucked in the back corner of the room. Pulling out a key that was strung on a necklace around her neck, she unlocked a drawer and pulled out a small slip of paper.

"This is for you."

Clare took it and unfolded it.

"Though truth often varies, the heart never tarries; a stone is found, whence it is born."

"Oh, a riddle that makes little sense. Fantastic," Clare said, raising an eyebrow at Branna, who just shrugged.

"It is believed that a riddle will fall into place at the right time," Branna said sweetly.

"Thanks, I think. Listen, we have to get going, so, if I don't see you for a while…" Clare blinked back the tears that welled up again. Branna pulled Clare to her in a tight hug and Clare buried her face in Branna's hair for a moment. She smelled like lavender and honey, and her touch instantly soothed Clare. She wondered for a moment if Branna had soothed her nerves with magick.

"*Ádh mór ort*," Branna said, wishing Clare luck.

"We'll need it. I'll be in touch," Clare said, then stood back as Branna hugged Bianca too.

"There are two leather pouches on the counter. Take them with. They'll be useful at some point," Branna instructed as they pushed through the bead curtain.

"You're a blessing, you are, Branna," Clare called back to her as they swept the leather pouches into their packs, stashing them away without looking at the contents.

"Goddess, please protect them on their journey," Branna said to the empty store.

CHAPTER 16

"Why do you think he told us to go to the chemist? Isn't that kind of weird?" Bianca asked as they hustled through the rain that had begun to fall in a steady sheet. Clare considered getting a taxi, but seeing as how she didn't know when she'd next be gainfully employed, it was best that they conserve their money.

"Maybe he moonlights as a chemist when he's not busy protecting the world from evil," Clare muttered, pulling her knit cap down further on her head. She'd braided her curls into one long strand that fell down her back, thus controlling some of the frizz the rain would tease out of her unruly hair.

"Hmm, so saving humans from disease and death," Bianca mused. "I like it."

Clare slanted a glance at her, but said nothing. They came to a stop in front of the chemist's shop. From the outside, it appeared to be a normal shop with narrow windows advertising various cold and flu remedies. But the more Clare studied it, the more she realized that something was off.

"Look, the door isn't made of glass. And the windows are lined with a white backing – see?" Clare pointed. "So you can't be seeing inside."

"It's a front," Bianca gasped.

"I'd bet my life on it," Clare agreed and tugged her friend's arm to hurry her around the brownstone and into the small alleyway in the back.

"Should we knock or something?" Bianca wondered as they stood beneath the glow of a hooded safety light, their shoulders hunched against the rain.

In answer, the door swung open.

"Ladies, come on in," Blake said, holding the door open. Clare wondered how he'd known they were in the back alley, and glanced quickly behind her to see if there were any cameras. Seeing none, she stepped through the door and paused. It felt like she had passed through a thin membrane of sorts. She raised an eyebrow in question at Blake.

"My wards," Blake said quietly.

Clare nodded. It seemed she was going to have to suspend all of her scientific skepticism and start learning – fast.

"You'll teach me." It wasn't a question, but an order. Blake seemed to positively bristle at the command.

"My job is to protect you," Blake bit out, crossing his

arms across his chest. He'd taken his leather coat off and now wore a faded forest green plaid shirt, the sleeves rolled up his forearms. Clare wasn't surprised to see intricate tattoos winding their way around his forearms, but she was annoyed by the immediate punch of lust that hit her at the sight of him.

"Sorry, Doc, my only job is to keep you alive. Not to be your teacher in all things magickal."

"Sorry, Mr. Security, but it's 2016 and women work with men in teams now. It's called being partners. And since you're coming along on this journey whether you like it or not, you'd better saddle up and teach me some damn magick," Clare hissed. Then she turned at Bianca's squeal.

Racing up the few steps into the front room, Clare skidded to a halt as she saw what her friend was making such a fuss about.

It was Seamus, but not Seamus. At least not the Seamus she'd known and grown to care deeply about over the past year and a half. Instead, he smiled sheepishly at her, a faint violet hue tinging his presence.

"You've got to be kidding me," Clare whispered, feeling her heart begin to pound wildly in her chest. First Branna, now Seamus. How long had fae been following her? How long had her life been in the control of others – all while she'd thought she'd been the captain of her own destiny and succeeding on her own?

"Sit," Blake ordered, reading her correctly, and pulled a chair out. Pushing down on her shoulders, he shoved her unceremoniously into the chair and pressed her head between her knees as she began to take wildly gulping breaths, trying to calm the panic that threatened to overtake her.

"I'm sorry, Clare, it's the truth that I am," Seamus said softly from across the room. "I'd've told you if I could've."

Clare waved her hand at him as she focused on her breathing. Same story, different person.

"Drink this," Blake said, handing her a small glass of amber liquid. Presuming it to be a shot of Irish, Clare downed it in one gulp, and found that her assumption was correct. As the liquor screamed its way down to her gut, she took another deep breath and met Seamus's eyes.

"I'm not mad at you. It's just, it's awful to be feeling I've been a pawn in some game my whole life. I've always felt like I've done well for myself. I've studied hard, been awarded scholarships, have been working myself to the bone for my future. And for what? My future was written a long time ago," Clare said bitterly, head in her hands.

"You still earned all that on your own. Nobody can take that away from you," Blake said, surprising her with a moment of kindness. Clare met his eyes and measured him for a moment.

"Aye, you're right at that, I suppose. Learning is learning, and that can never be taken away. Enough of the pity party, we might as well start strategizing our trip."

"Our trip?" Blake asked.

"You, me, Bianca, and Seamus. You can't think I'm doing this alone?" Clare asked in disbelief.

"Ah, well, traditionally, yes, it was most likely meant to be a solitary quest." Seamus cleared his throat and then ran his hand through his hair, causing the already spiky mess to stand up even more.

"Screw tradition," Clare said, standing up and stripping off her leather coat. "Tradition hasn't been working so well if the treasures haven't been found. Is there anything in this infamous legend that dictates I have to do this on my own?"

Seamus slid a glance at Blake and then met Clare's eyes again. There was a note of cheerfulness this time as he said, "Nope, absolutely nothing that says you can't. I think everyone's always assumed it's a solitary quest. But nothing in the rules about it."

"Right, brilliant," Clare muttered and then put her hands on her hips. Turning, she met everyone's eyes, one at a time. "Are you with me?"

"I'm so in," Bianca said immediately.

"I'm in," Seamus said quickly.

Which left Blake, standing there and measuring her with his blue eyes. Anger rolled from him in waves.

"I don't have much choice, do I? I'm sent to protect you," Blake bit out.

"Doesn't protecting me mean you'd have to follow me anyway?" Clare asked.

"*Na Cosantoir* stay hidden," Blake said.

"Well, you've broken that rule twice now, yourself,

haven't you? I can keep screaming for Domnua too, if you'd like," Clare said sweetly and was rewarded with a flash in his eyes.

"I'm in. But let it be noted that this is under duress."

"So noted," Clare said dryly. "Not that it matters when we save the world. Then I bet you'll be the first to ride the float in the parade."

A smile quirked the edges of Blake's mouth and Clare caught herself almost smiling in response. Instead, she turned and surveyed Seamus.

"So? Seamus? I'm assuming you're the brains here. Might as well get us started."

"Now you're just being bitchy," Bianca said, moving to take a seat next to Seamus. Clare's mouth dropped open at this betrayal from her best friend, but then she clamped her lips shut, stifling a sigh. If they were going to be a team, it wouldn't do to take shots at one another.

"I'm sorry," Clare said stiffly to Blake.

He nodded once at her. "I'm going downstairs. Feel free to start without me." And with preternatural speed, he was gone from the room.

"What's in the basement?" Bianca asked, craning her head after him.

"His lair," Seamus quipped.

"I wouldn't be surprised," Clare said, pulling up a chair in front of a sleek laptop. "Seamus, it's just killing me that you and Branna have been in on this all along. I'm going to need some time to absorb this."

"Please just know it was out of protection for you – not trying to lie to you," Seamus said immediately.

"I understand," Clare said, pulling her cap from her head and stuffing it in the sleeve of her coat. "It's just a shock, that's all." She tugged the band from her braid and began combing her hands through her hair, shaking out her mass of auburn curls. Blake entered the room in mid-shake and their eyes met and locked for one burning hot second. Clare felt the punch of his heat, searing its way through her whole body, and the promise of him made her heart ache.

Tearing his eyes away from her tumble of curls, Blake addressed the room.

"I've some notes that will help."

CHAPTER 17

*I*t wasn't so much notes as a leather envelope filled with sheaves of paper that probably dated back further than Clare wanted to know.

"What is this? Gaelic?" Clare said, holding one piece up in a gloved hand. Blake had insisted they wear gloves when handling the paper, and Clare couldn't tell if it was to protect the paper from the oils on their hands, or to protect them from the magick that seemed to pulse from the pages. She supposed it didn't matter either way.

Seamus craned his neck and looked at the paper she held. "Fae," he said cheerfully.

Clare's eyebrows rose as she studied the strange symbols. They were delicate and whimsical, yet jagged and sharp at the same time.

"I hadn't realized they had their own language. Though, if we're being truthful here, I didn't think your kind existed prior to today," Clare laughed at Seamus.

"Your kind too," Blake grumbled. Clare swung around to look at where he worked quietly in a corner.

"Excuse me?"

"Your kind too. You're part fae. A Danula. You'd have to be, in order to find the stone." Blake said this as though Clare were a complete idiot for not having figured this out sooner.

"I thought my powers," Clare held her fingers up in quotation marks, "were strictly related to the stone."

"They probably are. But who knows? You've not tested them and you've only let yourself believe in magick for a day now, so I'm sure there's more we will be seeing," Blake said dryly.

Clare narrowed her eyes at him. "It's not my fault I didn't believe in magick."

"Isn't it though?" Blake shot back. "You could've saved us all a lot of time if you'd opened your mind up a little sooner. Now, the clock is ticking."

Clare blinked back the tears that threatened, surprised to find herself wounded by his words. What did she care if he was annoyed with her? His job was to protect her. Period. Not to cast judgment on how she got to this place.

"Blake, you know *Na Sirtheoir* are chosen very carefully. It was destined that she figure this out in her own time and in her own way. Who is to say what would have happened if she had discovered her magick years ago before any of us found her and were able to put safeguards in place for her?" Seamus asked.

Clare scrubbed her hands over her eyes.

"It is astonishing to me that you've been aware of me for so long. Have you been protecting me my whole life?" Clare asked, directing the question at Blake.

"No," Blake said, not elaborating further.

"For a year then?" Clare pressed the issue.

Blake's gaze seared into hers as he held her eyes.

"I've been protecting you since you've come to Dublin," Blake finally bit out.

Clare's heart skipped a beat. For almost a decade then, this man had been following her. Was this why she felt so drawn to him? So connected? Had she seen him at some point and never registered it?

"Why… why didn't you ever approach me?" Clare whispered.

"That's not how it works. We're supposed to stay hidden. Things took too long, the Domnua made moves too quickly, and, well, here we are," Blake shrugged, but Clare could feel the anger that vibrated through him.

"And you blame me," Clare said, shoving back from the table and stalking from the room. She slammed the door to the small bathroom Seamus had shown the girls earlier, and clutched the edges of the sink as she stared into the mirror. Who was this person looking back at her? And just what was she capable of? Clare tried to calm her breathing as she looked at all angles of the problem.

Somehow, they would need to pull together as a team. And there was more of a problem between her and Blake than between anyone else. And so, if she must be the leader – then she would lead.

Stepping from the bathroom, Clare stood in the doorway to the front room.

"Blake, I'd like to speak to you alone," Clare ordered, her voice sharp.

Bianca's eyebrows shot up to her hairline, but she kept quiet and busied herself with writing a note on a pad of paper in front of her. Seamus observed them both with interest.

"Is now really the time for this?" Blake asked, a mulish expression on his face.

"Aye, now is the time for it," Clare said, her shoulders held back.

"Fine. Downstairs," Blake ordered, trying to take charge of the situation again. Clare simply turned and, by instinct, wound her way through a hallway and to a doorway. Reaching out, she turned the handle and found it was locked.

Clare stiffened as she felt Blake's warmth at her back. He reached over her shoulder and pressed his hand to a spot on the wall. His breath was warm at her neck, and it took all of Clare's power not to shiver in response.

The door slid noiselessly open, surprising Clare as it had looked like the type that would swing open. More magick, she thought.

Blake nudged her gently, his hand at her back, his heat searing her through the thin fabric of her sweater. She jumped and all but ran down the steps. When she arrived at the bottom she turned her head back and forth, trying to take in everything the room held at once.

Where she'd expected a dark lair of sorts – in keeping with his dark attire – she was proven wrong by the brightly lit room. Three different cream-painted doors set off sage green walls and white trim. A few rugs were thrown across dark wood floors, and two cream couches with navy blue pillows created a conversation area. In one corner, a full curved bar with a gleaming white marble countertop had several metal stools positioned in front of it. Overall it was warm, modern, and far sleeker than anything she had expected from him. Stepping forward, she trailed her hand over the back of a cream leather couch.

"Decorate this yourself, did you?" Clare asked, finally turning to meet Blake's eyes. One thing noticeably missing from the room was any sign of personal effects. If anything, it was a perfectly staged living area. Her eyes wandered to one of the doors. She wondered what else was hidden down here.

"I had a say in the decorating," Blake said as he crossed to the bar. Clare felt an instant stab of jealousy as she wondered if one of Blake's girlfriends had helped him decorate. And wasn't that a new and troubling thought?

"Are you dating someone?" Clare asked straight out and then fought to keep a blush from rising to her cheeks.

Standing behind the bar pouring a splash of whiskey into each of two glasses, Blake paused. Turning to glance at her over his shoulder, he smiled – a wolf scenting his prey.

"And if I am?"

"No matter to me. I just wondered if you had a

female help with the decorating touches. And, well, I suppose it's best to know if any jealous women are going to chase us down and interrupt our quest," Clare added quickly.

"No jealous females to interrupt the quest," Blake said, walking forward to hand her a glass. Clare sipped the whiskey, realizing that he hadn't answered the question she'd really been asking.

She'd do well to stay on her toes around Blake; he was far smarter than he let on.

"Care to have a seat?" Blake asked, gesturing to a couch.

"Yes, that'll be fine," Clare said, moving around the edge of the couch and sitting on the one that lined the wall. It surprised her when Blake sat beside her and not across the table from her. In doing so, he positioned himself as her equal – as someone who wanted to take the lead on this mission. It made her bristle.

"And?" Blake asked, gesturing with his glass. A hint of humor slid through his eyes and she knew that he was amused with her annoyance.

"Yes, well, as leader of this team, I felt it was best that I address some problem areas before we go much further along on this quest," Clare said, pulling her shoulders back and meeting his eyes. He'd turned so that his leg was almost brushing hers and his arm was thrown along the back of the couch – his hand but inches away from touching her hair. Realizing it, Clare quickly swept her hair over her shoulder and away from his hand.

"I see," Blake said, taking another sip and watching her quietly.

Clare waited and then almost rolled her eyes. "So, you know, if you could just go ahead and stop with the blaming me shite, that'd be great. It's not my fault that I didn't know any of this until two days ago. I've worked for everything that I've had in my life and it hasn't been easy." Clare was shocked to hear a hitch in her voice, but she powered through. "I kept my head down and did my work and when I wasn't studying, I was juggling jobs. So excuse me if I didn't have time to pay attention to magick. But I don't appreciate you taking your frustration out on me. If you were watching me for ten damn years, then what the hell were you doing? Why didn't you leave me a damn message so I could get up to speed? This is as much your fault as it is mine. More so yours! At least you were given the rule book. I had nothing." Clare bit off the last words bitterly and eyed Blake as he calmly leaned over and pulled the whiskey glass from her hand.

Her mouth dropped as he placed the two glasses gently on the table in front of them. What on earth was he doing?

Seconds later, his lips were on hers and his hands were threaded deep into her hair, his kiss a violent assault, so pained, so deep, that she writhed against him – both pushing him away and pulling him back to her. On some deep level that she wasn't ready to acknowledge, Clare knew she'd been waiting for this.

And oh, the promise his eyes held was a thousand times hotter in the flesh, with his lips pressed against hers, his body pinning her to the couch. His kiss tasted of years of pent-up anger and lust, ravaging her and leaving her body crying out for more.

Blake tore away and cursed, low and steady, as he ran his hand through his hair. Clare gasped for breath, her mind frozen by the swirl of emotions that still raced through her.

"I didn't contact you because of that," Blake spit out, reaching out and downing the rest of his whiskey in one gulp. Clare watched him in fascination, his words finally registering through the haze of lust that clouded her brain.

"Of that?" Clare squeaked, clearing her throat as she unconsciously licked her lower lip. Blake cursed again and stood up, pacing the center of the room.

"Yes, this. You. This attraction I've had. It's not right, that's the long and short of it. It's not right at all."

"It's not... why isn't it right?" Clare was trying to keep up, but she was distracted by the way his fitted jeans molded to his thighs, his butt, his...

"You. And me!" Blake all but shouted and Clare focused on the problem at hand. "I'm supposed to protect you. It is my destiny to protect you. That doesn't mean lust after you."

"You've lusted after me?" Clare asked, honestly shocked.

Blake's eyes met hers, and for the very first time, she saw a hint of vulnerability there.

"For years, I've watched you. Go to school, work at the pub, kiss other men – when, goddess above, your lips should have been on mine. Your beauty, your brains – your skin… ah, it all but glows from within. When you shake your curls out, it looks like fire rippling down your back and I want to bury my hands in your hair and myself deep within your body."

Clare lost all capacity for speech as his words registered; she quite simply could not think of even a word to say in response. All she knew was that she wanted his hands on her body again.

"And you sit there… you sit there, your eyes wide as saucers, licking your lips, all but begging me to take you where you sit. You see why I'm angry? How can I protect you if you're a constant distraction? I need to speak to someone. Find someone else to protect you. I knew it would be a disaster should I ever show myself to you." Blake cursed again, his pace picking up, and Clare's annoyance shifted.

"Now wait just a minute. You don't get to be assigned to another case. You can't just drop this bomb on me and then try to back out. You've been protecting me for ten years and now you want to just walk away? Leave me like this?" Clare shook her head in astonishment. "Have you no honor?"

Blake leaped and had Clare pressed back against the cushions in less than a second.

"If I had no honor, I'd take what I wanted from you and leave."

A shiver of distaste ran through Clare, but she stilled

the words that sprang to her lips. Looking up, she searched his eyes; in them, she found the answer she needed.

"No, you wouldn't. Because you're my Protector," Clare said softly.

Blake bowed his head so that his forehead touched hers. "Aye, I'm your Protector."

"What do you need from me so you can do your job?" Clare finally asked, trying to stay focused, though she wanted to run her hands up the back of his shirt and feel the muscles stretched tight beneath it.

"I need you to trust me. And even if you want to lead, I need you to listen. You'll know when I mean it. Lead all you want, my fierce *Na Sirtheoir*, but listen too. That's all I ask."

Clare stared into his eyes, fascinated by the layers of blue found there, as though waves crashed over each other into a spiral of oceanic depths.

"Aye, I'll trust you."

Blake sighed, sliding his lips over hers in the briefest hint of a kiss, his tenderness more searing than his earlier assault. It made Clare want to whimper and beg for more. Instead, she allowed him to pull her from the couch and lead her back to the stairs. Turning, he looked down at her.

"You've much to learn yet. I fear I'll cloud your brain, and you mine. Can you understand why I need the distance?"

She understood what he was asking of her – even though it already hurt to know he wanted space.

"Aye, I'll keep my distance," Clare said softly, regret hanging on every word.

It just wasn't their time, she told herself as they climbed the stairs.

Maybe it never would be.

CHAPTER 18

*J*udging from the pink flush across Bianca's cheeks and her mussed blonde hair, Clare hadn't been the only one locking lips. Deciding it best to ignore any indication of amorous activities, Clare cleared her throat.

"Blake and I have worked through a few things. I feel we'll be able to move forward as a team without too many hiccups." Clare's gaze slid to Seamus, who winked at her with a cheeky grin on his face. "While I'll try to lead, it's been pointed out to me that there will be times when others will know best. Team Treasure it is."

Seamus whooped and shot his fist in the air. Then he pulled out a sheet of paper. "Clare, is it true that Branna gave you a clue?"

"Och, that's right." Clare shook her head and pulled the slip of paper from her pocket. Blake shook his head and looked up at the ceiling – but to his credit, he didn't say anything.

"Though truth often varies, the heart never tarries; a stone is found, whence it is born."

"Ah, my brethren. They do love a good riddle," Seamus said with a smile as he wrote the words down.

"Oh? You think this is great fun?" Clare asked, but found herself smiling at him.

"Keeps me brain ticking along." Seamus grinned at her again, the freckles standing out on his face as he flushed with excitement.

"Clare," Blake said, and Clare glanced over to where he sat by a computer.

"Yes?"

"What does your gut say about the riddle?"

"That I need to go to where I was born," Clare said immediately, then slapped a hand over her mouth, surprised at the words.

"To Clifden?" Bianca asked in surprise.

"I guess? That's what was in my gut." Clare shrugged, worrying now about seeing her family after all she had learned.

"Were you born in Clifden?" Blake asked and Clare opened her mouth to respond automatically, then paused.

"Well, I want to be saying yes. But sure and I think my gut is telling me no." Clare looked in disbelief at Bianca, who just shrugged a shoulder. There was no way she would know the answer.

"Methinks you're needing to have a wee chat with the parents," Seamus pointed out.

"But how could I not be born there? Our family has lived in Clifden for decades."

"Perhaps you were born on holiday somewhere and they brought you home right away," Bianca suggested.

"Why would someone go on holiday when they were about to have a baby?" Blake asked.

"Aye, that's a good point there. What woman wants to be away from home if she's going to be giving birth?"

"She could have been an early birth," Bianca pointed out, somewhat huffily.

"You're right. I could have been. I don't actually recall any stories about when I was born. That's weird, right? I should know how I was born. Don't most mothers like to hold that over your head? About how they spent three days laboring over your birth and you'd better take care of them in their old age?" Clare was speaking too fast but the panic she felt swirling around in her stomach was making the words just tumble out.

"Hey, slow down. It's all right, it is." Bianca came to Clare and wrapped her arm around her friend's shoulder.

"What if my parents aren't really my parents?" Clare breathed, looking into Bianca's eyes.

"That's just the silliest thing ever. Of course they're your parents," Bianca exclaimed. "They raised you, didn't they? Who taught you how to shear a sheep? And dig in the dirt for rocks? And who brags about you down the pub? And sends you knitted blankets and sweaters? Those are parents if I've ever seen them. Even if – even if we find out they didn't give birth to you. You hear me? They're still yours. Only you can let that be taken away from you. So, you know, just don't."

And that, it seemed, was that. Clare pulled Bianca in for a tight hug, because, really, there wasn't much else she could say.

Bianca was one hundred percent correct.

Blood didn't make the parents.

Love did.

Blake met her eyes from across the room.

"Looks like we're going for a drive."

"Road trip!" Bianca squealed.

CHAPTER 19

*O*f course he owned a Range Rover, Clare thought as they piled into the sleek black SUV that Blake pulled from some secret garage. Between the black leather jacket, the brooding good looks, and now the hot car, Clare was convinced Blake was doing his damnedest to make her sit up and beg.

Instead, she stretched nonchalantly on the smooth buttery leather in the front seat, purposely easing into the languidness of the stretch, hoping to drive him just a little bit crazy. When she caught, out of the side of her eye, the scowl that flashed across his face, she considered them to be even.

"Great car, Blake," Bianca said, all but bouncing up and down on the back seat. They were leaving later in the day than was probably prudent for a road trip, but they'd needed to pack bags and do the other mundane bits that came with planning for a journey. Bianca had been smart to pack a cooler of food and a picnic hamper, but she had always been a planner like that. Clare had bit her tongue when she'd seen the neat roll of sleeping bags and tents tucked into the corner of the storage area. If Blake thought they would be sleeping outside in the middle of January in Ireland, he had another thing coming.

"Thanks, Bianca. It's good to have a car like this, though I rarely drive it in the city. Something smaller suits tooling around Dublin."

"Neither of us even own a car," Clare admitted.

Blake slid her a glance.

"I know."

Of course he knew. He probably knew what kind of tampons she bought, and where she went to buy her lingerie. It was irritating and oddly attractive at the same time.

"Clare, are you ready for some lessons?" Seamus asked politely from the backseat.

She turned in her seat to look at him. "What type of lessons?"

"I think we had discussed seeing what other type of magick you hold? Or perhaps you just want sort of an oral history of magick? I'm not really sure where to start with you. Frankly, I'm surprised you're this far along. What with that science-focused mind of yours."

"I'm expanding my horizons," Clare declared. Blake snorted.

"Ah, well, that's a good thing, it is," Seamus said agreeably.

"Let's start with a history of the *Na Cosantoir*," Clare said sweetly and caught Blake's glare from the corner of her eye. Pleasure at annoying him swept through and she smiled brightly at Seamus.

"Is that really the best use of your time right now?" Bianca asked, ever the peacemaker.

"Shouldn't I know all the players in the game?" Clare countered.

"I'd think you'd be more interested in learning about the ones that are trying to end your existence on this earth," Blake pointed out.

"Sure and you don't think I can't learn about both now, do you?" Clare asked, tilting her head at him, all wide-eyed innocence.

"It's a four-hour drive to Clifden, depending on traffic. Would you rather explore your magick and learn something that could keep you from being harmed or help you find the stone – or are you more interested in uncovering my past?" Blake asked, his tone edging toward harshness.

Clare wondered if this was one of the times where when he said to trust him, she was supposed to. Figuring it wasn't worth the fight, and also somewhat curious to see if she did have magick, she sighed dramatically and winked at Seamus.

"Fine, magickal powers it is."

Seamus beamed at her and she smiled back, incredibly grateful to have him on this trip. She was beginning to get used to his violet glow – as weird as that sounded in her head.

"I can probably help with getting us started on my magickal powers," Clare admitted.

Bianca's mouth dropped open. "Have you been keeping something from me?"

"Not just you – everyone," Clare admitted, and saw her friend's face go stony. Reaching back, she squeezed Bianca's hand. "Please know it was because I couldn't understand it, and because it didn't make sense – in the real world or scientific world – I buried it."

Bianca sniffed and looked away before nodding stiffly.

"I… it's just that, I feel like I can hear stones talking to me." Clare rushed it out in one sentence before she chickened out. Even saying the words out loud made a blush creep up her cheeks and she turned to stare out at the passing countryside. They were already a good thirty minutes outside Dublin, and buildings had been left behind for hills and open land.

"Well, duh, you're the one chosen to find the stone treasure," Bianca snorted, and Clare jumped, turning around to raise an eyebrow at her friend.

"You don't think it sounds crazy?"

"Well, maybe before I knew what you were, I might have. But now that I know, I mean, well, duh, right?" Bianca elbowed Seamus and he nodded his agreement.

"The beautiful lady speaks the truth. The expectation is that you should have a natural way of conversing with stones. It'll lead you straight as an arrow on your path. If you couldn't discern the truth of a stone, well, the Domnua could charm one to make you think you'd found the treasure."

Dread sliced through her at the realization that she was most definitely in way over her head.

"It never occurred to me that the fae would make a fake stone. Are they really that cunning?" Clare asked softly.

Seamus let out a booming laugh that all but shook the car, slapping his leg hard as he laughed.

"Oh, my dear Clare, you're a balm for my jaded soul. Aye, of course fae are that cunning. They're known to be quite the tricksters. *We're* known to be," Seamus amended, catching her eyes, "or you would have known what I was ages ago."

"Here I have this big secret and nobody is surprised by it," Clare grumbled.

"If you teleported us to Clifden, I'd be surprised then," Blake said, but he shot Clare a smile to soften his words.

Fine, so they were teasing her. She needed to relax a bit.

"Tell me what you mean by 'stones talk to you,'" Bianca asked. "It looks like I'm the only non-magickal one here, so I'd like to know."

"You're magick to me, beautiful," Seamus said immediately, and the entire car paused for a moment.

"Awwww," they all said at once and burst into laughter.

"Stop it! Don't take my moment away from me," Bianca ordered, but she was laughing too.

"To answer your question – I can't quite say. For example, if someone comes to the shop with a particular ailment, I'll know which stone will help heal them. Not because of what books say, but because that stone will quite literally say to me, 'I'm the stone meant for this person.' It's not like I hear a voice in my head exactly, it's more that I just see the words in my mind. If that makes sense?"

"Sure and that makes perfect sense to me," Bianca said. "It's like using your intuition to the tenth degree."

"Something like that," Clare agreed. "And, well, the only other thing I'm aware of at this point is that I can now see fae."

"The colors show up for you now?" Blake asked, one arm on the wheel, looking relaxed in the driver's seat. Clare could almost – almost – imagine they were on their way to holiday instead of some sort of magickal mission.

"Aye, they do," Clare said.

"What colors? The silver eyes?" Bianca asked.

"Yes, and the violet glow of the Danula. Seamus has it," Clare said, and Bianca cast a speculative glance at him.

"You're purple?"

"Violet, thank you very much," Seamus sniffed.

"What color is Blake?" Bianca demanded.

Clare cast her eyes at him and studied him for a moment.

"I can't really tell. I almost want to say violet but then it fades to a white and then into nothing and he just looks normal."

"Normal is good," Blake said with a nod.

"He's almost pure white because he's fighting for the highest good of our gods and goddesses," Seamus interjected.

Clare sat back, stunned. "You're an angel?"

Blake snorted. "Do you see a halo?"

"Ah, well, you know," Seamus said, "we don't really have angels in our history. I suppose if you wanted to compare it to different religions, then he's an angel of sorts. Being a *Na Cosantoir* is a job of great honor."

"Like a knight? Oh, he's like a knight in shining armor! Except he glows instead of wearing armor!" Bianca gasped and then fanned her face dramatically. "It's so romantic."

"Hey, I'm a warrior too, you know," Seamus grumbled.

Bianca reached out and squeezed Seamus's leg. "Of course you are. I just… you know, the whole fairytale thing."

"I'll give you a fairytale," Seamus promised, and Bianca twinkled up at him.

"Moving on," Blake cleared his throat, but Clare caught a hint of a blush in his cheeks. "I suspect one of your magicks is to freeze."

Clare paused before speaking, confusion racing through her. "To freeze? Freeze time?"

Blake chuckled, his smile making his wickedly handsome face even more devastating. "Freeze motion."

"I don't understand," Clare asked. "Sure and you can't be saying I can freeze something in its tracks."

"Why, that makes sense," Seamus interrupted. "Because her treasure is stone, one of the closest elemental powers would be to freeze."

"Wouldn't the closest element be earth?" Bianca asked in confusion.

"It doesn't work like that. Fae world, weird rules, that kind of stuff," Seamus explained quickly. "I'm surprised that didn't occur to me earlier."

"Doesn't ice kill fae?" Bianca asked.

Seamus put his arm around her, squeezing her to him for a moment. "I love how your mind works. I wish you would've looked at me sooner. I've been crushing on that pretty face and brilliant mind for a year now."

"You have?" Bianca drew the word out in a long breath.

"I have. You're the light in my world," Seamus said and then turned back to Clare, leaving Bianca flustered in the back seat. "Freezing isn't icing someone, though it would be amazing if you could do that. Then you could just, zap, zap, zap... you're iced! And take down a Domnua."

Despite herself, Clare had to laugh at Seamus's enthusiasm.

"But really, what it does is it stops something that's in motion. A ball rolling, a Domnua attacking, that kind of thing. It's a sort of a pause button."

"How long does that last?" Clare asked, beside herself with curiosity. She flexed her hands in her lap and looked down at them, wondering if she really did hold such a power.

"Not long. Maybe enough to get your dagger into their heart. Perhaps enough to stop someone from being hit by a car. It's wise not to get cocky with it, because as soon as they unfreeze, they're coming for you like a freight train," Blake said, his tone and his words sending a chill through Clare.

"I, uh, I can't even think about sticking a dagger in someone's heart," Clare admitted helplessly. "It's so out of the realm of what I know. I'm not sure I'm really the right person for this quest."

"You'll feel differently when a Domnua's about to slice your head off, trust me," Seamus said cheerfully.

"Sure and you're joking with me," Clare said.

"Sadly, I'm not. I think tonight we'll need to work on some basic self-defense and sword work. For now, we can practice magick."

"How in the world can I practice magick in a moving car?" Clare exclaimed, turning to look at Seamus.

"Easy," Seamus said – and tossed a can of soda at her face.

Clare reacted without thinking, her hand coming up to block her face, but the can never reached her.

Instead, it hung suspended in the air.

Clare's eyes grew as wide as saucers. Seamus caught it neatly when it finally fell, stopping it from exploding all over the car.

"See? You're a natural."

CHAPTER 20

*A*fter a few panicky moments during which Clare had to put her head between her knees and take deep breaths, she began to practice. Though her science-mind refused to accept that the laws of physics could so easily be broken, that same mind marveled at how the magick worked. She wanted to dissect it and write a paper about it, look for formulas or explanations.

Blake had laughed at her when she'd said as much, but it had held no sting. He seemed to be willing to indulge her curiosity – much like a child learning to ride a bike for the first time – as she threw a pen repeatedly into the air in front of her and froze it in mid-air.

They'd stopped for a quick break outside Galway, where Blake had given them but minutes to use the restrooms. He was trying to limit their exposure to the public, as he was worried the Domnua would be tracking them. As far as they knew, the Domnua still thought Clare was in Dublin, but they couldn't be sure.

As they wound around a curve on the dark road, Clare raised a question that had been bothering her.

"How did they not know who I was? I mean, they know now – but one of you mentioned they had to find me. And how will they find the next? Do we know who the next girl is?" Seamus had already explained that all *Na Sirtheoir* were women.

"That's part of the Goddess protecting you. If the Domnua could figure out who you were, they'd kill you when you were a defenseless baby. There is a protection in place until you are much older," Blake explained.

"Is that why my parents never saw my mark – the one on my head?" Clare asked.

"When the mark comes out, the protection has been lifted and you are on your own. Aside from the Protectors and the Danula watching out for you, that is. But even the Danula must find you first. I've been with you since as soon as the mark showed."

Clare shook her head, still marveling at how long Blake had been protecting her while she had remained oblivious.

"Do I have a color?" Clare exclaimed, suddenly realizing that this must be how the fae discerned what she was.

"You do," Blake smiled at her, appreciating that she had finally picked up on it.

"Well, what is it?" Clare demanded.

"Gold," Blake and Seamus said at the same time.

Clare gasped, looking down at herself. She couldn't detect the color anywhere. "I'm gold?"

"A nice shiny gold. It's a lovely color with your skin tone and auburn locks," Seamus said easily.

"But why gold?"

"Fae love shiny things. Gold is one of the most coveted metals. Since you are, you know, one of the elite – a *Na Sirtheoir* – well, you get gold as your color."

"I guess that takes the phrase 'you're good as gold' to a whole new level," Bianca quipped. They all laughed, though Clare was having trouble absorbing all these new ideas. It was like her identity had shifted and she was being forced to see herself through an entirely different lens. It wasn't bad or good, she supposed; it just was. Being a somewhat pragmatic sort, she'd learned to not question things she couldn't change.

And it seemed being a Seeker was something she had no choice about.

Narrowing her eyes at the thought, she turned to Blake.

"Do I have a choice in being a Seeker? Can I just renounce it and go back to living my normal life?"

"Sure, for as long as the Domnua would let you live," Blake said.

"They'd still try to kill me? Even if I wasn't seeking the treasure?"

"Aye."

"Well, that's just shitty," Clare murmured, her eyes scanning the dark road ahead of them.

"That's the way of things, I guess," Blake agreed.

"Where are we staying tonight? As I've yet to tell my parents we're coming."

"I've got us a place to stay about twenty minutes out."

"You aren't thinking we'll be sleeping in those sleeping bags, are you?"

Blake grinned, his teeth a flash of white in the light from the console. "Not tonight, but one of these nights, most likely."

"You realize it's the thick of winter, right?" Bianca interjected from the back seat.

"You realize we're trying to save the world, right?" Blake parroted back.

"I suppose it's a small matter when you put it like that," Bianca grumbled.

CHAPTER 21

The headlights of the Range Rover washed over what looked like a small farmhouse with two cottages tucked behind it. A light shone in the front window of the farmhouse and Clare saw the shadow of a figure move.

"Be right back," Blake said, hopping out of the car and leaving it running. He jogged to the front door, which had already opened, but the figure stayed shadowed and Clare couldn't make out much more. In moments, Blake had returned to the car, keys dangling from his hand.

"Both of the cottages are ours, so we'll be sleeping here tonight," Blake said, pulling the Range Rover around the house and driving it toward the stone cottages. A small light shone from the front of each, illuminating the cheerful blue doors, but the rest remained in darkness.

"Girls' and boys' cabins?" Clare said lightly, though

her heart had picked up speed when Blake had mentioned only two cottages.

"Nice try, Doc. You'll be bunking with me."

"Why can't I sleep with Bianca?" Clare demanded.

"I, for one, would certainly have no problem with that – so long as I could watch," Seamus piped up from the back seat. Bianca squealed and smacked him across the shoulder.

"You'll be staying where I can keep an eye on you. I'll ask that you not make this more difficult than it has to be," Blake said evenly, but Clare could read the steel beneath his words.

"Fine. You may sleep on the floor," Clare said evenly, getting out of the car to put an end to the conversation. Blake's chuckle followed her, and a shiver worked its way down her spine.

"Are you sure you're okay with staying with him?" Bianca grabbed her hand and whispered in her ear. "I mean, I would be, 'cause, duh, he's delicious. But I don't want to put you in an uncomfortable situation."

Clare glanced over to where Blake stood hefting several bags easily from the trunk.

"I can handle him."

"Mmhm, I bet you can."

"What about you? Do you have a problem bunking with Seamus?"

"He isn't going to know what hit him," Bianca declared. Clare laughed, long and hard. Both men looked over at them, but Clare just pulled Bianca in for a hug.

"So much for letting him woo you," Clare quipped.

"See? I told you they wanted to sleep together," Seamus said, making Clare laugh even harder.

"Try and get some rest," Clare cautioned her friend and breezed past Seamus with a cheeky grin on her face. His eyebrows rose at her look, but then his gaze sought Bianca and he hurried after her toward their own cottage.

"Your accommodations await, madam," Blake said dryly, swinging the cottage door open. Clare breezed past him with her nose in the air.

The cottage was essentially one big room, with a small kitchenette on one side, a table with two chairs, and a queen-sized bed tucked under the eaves on the other end. A threadbare circle rug covered worn wood floors, and a small couch lined one wall. A door next to the bed led to what Clare hoped was a bathroom.

Though there wasn't much decoration, the cottage was quaint and serviceable, which held its own type of charm.

"Is this a bed and breakfast?"

"Something like that," Blake said, tossing his bag onto the couch and stretching. Clare found herself staring at the way his muscles rippled under his shirt, and turned away to put her bag on the bed and dig through it for her toiletry bag. Her hand stilled as she realized that she hadn't brought any decent pajamas with her. Typically she just slept in her underwear and a t-shirt or a tank top. Silently cursing herself, Clare turned and narrowed her eyes at him.

"I hope you don't think you'll be sleeping in the same

bed as me," she declared, sticking her nose up in the air again.

"I believe I was the one who said I didn't need the distraction," Blake pointed out, not looking up from digging through his bag.

"I'm aware. I was making sure you still understood where I stand," Clare said, then swept into the tiny bathroom. Slamming her bag onto the sink, she glared at herself in the mirror. One moment this man had her blind with lust and the next he infuriated her. This hot and cold game was never one that she'd played well, Clare reminded herself. She had chased after a few bad boys in her life. She would be smart to remember what they were all fighting for.

And it certainly wasn't for love.

Her eyebrows rose as the word slipped through her mind and settled low in her gut. Love? There was no way she could love a man she'd just met. Just because she'd felt an instant connection with him certainly didn't mean it was love.

Or even that he felt the same way back. Protecting her for years was his duty. Admiring her from afar was probably just a consequence of his vocation – not something she should read into.

"Everything okay in there?" Blake called and Clare jumped.

"Yes, I'll be but a moment," Clare called. She quickly washed her face, brushed her teeth, and used the toilet tucked next to a small shower stall in the corner. At least there was a shower, Clare thought.

Taking her bra off but leaving her jeans on and tugging a loose t-shirt over her head, Clare finished up. Stepping from the bathroom, she screamed as a pillow came flying at her head.

Instinctively, she threw her hands up and froze the pillow in mid-air, the magick seeming to flow from her very core, warming her, and out through the tips of her fingers. She couldn't see it – but she felt it.

It was weird that, all along, she'd held this magick inside. And yet she had never once had a glimmer of it – aside from when she was near stones.

"Sorry, but I needed to test you," Blake said, stooping and picking up the contents of her toiletry bag from where they had scattered across the floor. Pausing, he held up a foil packet, and Clare blushed from her hairline all the way down to the tips of her toes.

"We'll not be needing that," Clare said succinctly, grabbing it from his hand and shoving it back into her bag. She kept her back turned as she buried the small toiletry bag deep within her knapsack and worked desperately to calm her embarrassment.

"I've cut up an apple and have some biscuits here if you'd like a little snack before bed," Blake said.

Clare turned, pushing her braid over her shoulder. "Thanks," she said. She crossed the room and picked up a couple of biscuits, a slice of apple, and a bottle of water sitting on the table. Turning, she stomped back to the bed,

then curled up by the headboard. Leaning over, she put her
food on the bedside table – aside from the slice of apple,
which she shoved in her mouth – and snagged her phone
from her purse. Pulling it out, she pointedly ignored Blake
as she began to scroll through Facebook to see what else
was going on in the world.

And almost choked on her apple when the phone was
yanked from her hand.

"Hey!" Clare said, coughing as she tried to clear her
throat. Swallowing, she glared up at Blake who towered
over her side of the bed.

"You can't use your phone."

"Why the hell not?" Clare asked.

"Fae love electronics. They'll track you quite easily. I
should have told you to turn it off earlier." Blake cursed
long and low as he turned her phone off and handed it back
to her. Clare looked at the small, seemingly innocuous,
white iPhone like it was a grenade.

"They can do that?"

"Yes," Blake said simply, then turned and went back to
the table. He sat and focused on his food, making small
notes on a pad of paper. Silence filled the room, and with
nothing to distract her, Clare began to get antsy.

"Any other rules I should know about, oh wise one?"
Clare finally asked.

"Don't wander off on your own. Tell me where you're
going at all times. Don't use electronics. I'm always right,
you're always wrong. That should cover it."

She almost threw a pillow at him. But, deciding to be

an adult, she restrained herself. "I'm going to sleep. You're sleeping on the couch."

Blake looked up at that, glancing at the couch – which was clearly too small for his large frame – and then back at her.

"No, I'm not. But you're welcome to sleep there. It will fit your size better."

Stuck, Clare stared him down mulishly. She really didn't want to sleep on the couch. But she didn't trust herself to sleep in the same bed as him. Angry, she pulled the top blanket off of the bed and grabbed a pillow. Refusing to meet his eyes, she walked to the couch. Crawling onto it, she pulled the blanket over herself to hide her body while she slid her jeans off. Pulling them out, she hung them over the arm of the couch, then turned toward the back of the couch, punching a cushion to adjust herself better. Lumpy and made of a scratchy fabric, the couch was not suited for sleeping.

"I'd appreciate it if you'd turn the light off," Clare finally said, so angry at the situation that she wanted to scream.

"Yes, dear. I'm just going to get ready for bed."

Clare rolled her eyes as she heard him use the bathroom, then almost jumped when she heard the clink of his belt and the zip of his pants. It took all of her willpower not to turn around and take a peek. Instead, she pulled the thin blanket further over her head and prayed that sleep would come quickly.

Or even at all.

CHAPTER 22

*B*lake shook his head at her stubbornness as he slid under the covers of the bed. For someone who carried a condom in her toiletry bag, she certainly was a prude about sharing a bed. He could just see the red-gold sheen of her hair in the sliver of light that he'd left on in the bathroom.

It was taking every ounce of his willpower not to walk over to the couch and yank the blanket off of her. He'd almost wept in delirium when he'd seen her jeans come out from beneath the blanket.

He supposed that was what happened after a self-imposed celibacy. There were no rules about being celibate while being a Protector. But it hadn't taken long after he'd first seen Clare for him to realize that there was no other woman for him.

Instead, he'd channeled his lust and angst into spending long hours at the gym, and into ruthlessly killing any Domnua that got within a city's range of Clare. Now that her time had come, though, there were too many Domnua for him to handle on his own. It was best that they left.

Clare made a noise in her sleep, making him sit up a bit to examine the bundle on the couch. Was she sleeping or was she crying? He held his breath as he listened.

When another whimper came from the blanket, he slid from the bed and padded over to the couch. Silently, he stood over her. When she squirmed and whimpered again, he realized she was having a bad dream. Without another thought, he bent and picked her up, cradling her in his arms as he went back to the bed.

Clare didn't wake as he placed her gently in the bed, still wrapped in the blanket, and pulled the covers over them both. Instead, she whimpered again and turned and wrapped her arms around him.

Blake's eyes widened and he glanced down to see if he could see the gleam of her eyes in the light from the bathroom. But no; she still slept.

Blake sighed and wrapped an arm around her shoulders, while she burrowed even closer into his side. At least she wasn't whimpering anymore.

Resigning himself to a night of no sleep, Blake stared up at the rafters and began to plan their next step.

Which turned out to be a blessing. Had he been sleeping, he would have missed the Domnua who slid through the thin crack at the bottom of the cottage's door.

CHAPTER 23

A noise like a keening wail woke Clare with a jerk. Disoriented, she looked around as shadows writhed in the sliver of light that fell from the bathroom.

Remembering where she was, but confused as to why she was on the bed, she squealed as she saw Blake's arm come up and drive a dagger through a shadowy being. A shock of silver light, a flow of liquid silver to the floor, and she suddenly realized they were under attack.

Scrambling up from the bed, Clare pushed open the bathroom door so that the whole cottage was illuminated. Blake turned in a circle, his eyes resting on her for only a second as he continued to scan.

"The window over the sink!" Clare squealed, having caught a glimpse of another shadowy something. Blake whirled and moved at his superhuman speed across the room, his dagger flashing in the light just before another shock of silvery light slid to the floor.

Blake turned and paced the room, flipping on lights as he went, checking in every nook and cranny he could find.

Holding her hand to her throat, Clare decided now was not the time to comment on the fact that Blake was stark naked.

But, my, what a sight he was to behold, Clare thought, as her eyes traveled over the intricate tattoos that snaked up his arms, down his back, and across his deeply muscular chest. Her eyes followed one particularly interesting tattoo that led right to his navel.

"Look your fill?" Blake asked and Clare gasped, tearing her eyes away to rush past him and grab her jeans from the couch.

"Why was I in the bed?" Clare demanded, changing the subject and forcing the embarrassment down.

"You were having a bad dream," Blake said as he pulled his pants on – without any underwear, Clare noted. He began shoving their stuff in bags. "Get packed. We need to get out."

Perhaps she should have realized sooner that they were still in a precarious situation, Clare thought as she rushed to shove her things in her bag. She pulled her jacket over her t-shirt and her knapsack to her shoulders. When a shout sounded from outside, Clare gasped.

"Bianca and Seamus."

"Follow me out, your back to mine. Take this," Blake said, tossing a sheathed knife at her. Surprising herself, Clare caught it. Testing the weight in her hand, she pulled the knife from its sheath, the blade glinting in the light.

Oddly enough, it felt right in her hand. Not stopping to consider why, she followed Blake into the early dawn, her back to his as they made their way, step by step, to the other cottage.

With only the faint promise of light on the horizon, the yard was swathed in darkness; the only sound was the light kick of wind across the hills. Adrenaline surged through Clare and she narrowed her eyes, scanning the yard, trying to pick up on anything.

A streak of silver flashed across the yard and Clare hissed.

"Left!"

Blake pivoted and sliced through the streak, and the same flash of light and puddle of liquid silver followed. And wasn't that fascinating? The Domnua glowed in the dark. Pleased that she would be able to pick them out at any time of the night, Clare began to feel a little more confident.

Until she realized that if she could see them – they could see her.

The thought sobered her quickly, taking her newfound confidence down just a notch, as they worked their way rapidly to the nearby cottage. Just as they reached the door, Clare paused.

"Blake."

"What?"

"The horizon," Clare whispered, and Blake turned, immediately putting Clare behind him.

The Domnua Blake had just killed must have been sent

as a test. Because just clearing the ridge behind the cottages was a faint light, as though the sun were rising. But instead of golden rays brushing over the horizon, silver shot out.

"Get in the cottage," Blake ordered.

"I can't just leave you here," Clare exclaimed. "I'll fight too."

Blake turned and opened the door, shoving Clare into Seamus's arms.

"Hold her."

"Blake!" Clare shouted, but he was already gone from sight, racing into the horde of silver beings that careened over the hill.

"Bianca, hold Clare. Blake needs me to fight," Seamus said, turning and shoving Clare into Bianca's arms.

"I can't just stay here," Clare shouted as Seamus ran from the cottage, a silver sword in his hand. Seamus brandishing a sword was a sight in its own right, but Clare only had eyes for Blake as he slashed his way through fae after silvery fae.

"We aren't really going to let them fight this on their own, are we?" Bianca asked cheerfully. Clare's head whipped around to look at her friend. With two daggers in her hands and wearing a leather coat Clare had never seen before, Bianca looked prepared for battle.

"You're not going to force me to stay in here?"

"Since when have we ever let the boys do the fighting for us?" Bianca asked. "Let's show these boys that we can hold our own," she added, and raced into the dawn, Clare one step behind her.

Clare's heart stopped in her throat. There were just too many. It seemed as though they poured in from a never-ending spout. When one went down, the next flowed over the hill. Clare winced as Blake took another out, but not before the Domnua scored a hit on his arm.

"Maybe now would be a good time to use that freeze-frame magick trick?" Bianca asked – then squealed and drove her knife into something behind Clare's back.

Clare didn't have to look behind her to know that a silver puddle lined the ground.

"Nice catch. Can you see them now? And good call on the freezing," Clare muttered, turning to where the worst of the battle raged. Holding her hands out – and she wasn't sure why she did, but she'd seen it in the movies – she mentally shot her magick at the Domnua.

"Well, what the heck? Sure and you're right…I can see them now, just a glimmer of something," Bianca exclaimed, pivoting in excitement, "I wonder if it's because I slept with Seamus."

Clare stopped for a moment to consider those words, but forced herself to refocus on the more critical situation at hand.

Seamus paused as the Domnua that had just leaped at him froze in mid-air.

"That's a girl, Clare, right bloody brilliant of you," Seamus called and made short work of seven frozen

Domnua next to him. Blake, with his otherworldly speed, worked his way steadily through the crowd. Whenever they began to unfreeze, Clare just threw another bolt of magick at them.

"Back here!" a voice yelled, and Clare whipped around to see a woman in a white nightgown race from the back of the farmhouse and slice a fae through the heart.

From her pale violet glow, Clare could discern she was a Danula.

Bianca paced the yard with Clare, circling her constantly as Clare steadied her breathing and focused on freezing anything that dared to step into her line of vision.

Moments later, stillness greeted them, the only sound that of heavy breathing from Blake and Seamus.

"Are we clear then?" Clare called, still circling with Bianca.

"Aye, my wards aren't signaling anymore," the woman called, coming forward and wiping her dagger on her nightgown.

"I'm Morrigan. I apologize that this happened on my property. I had thought my wards were intact but it seems they figured out a way around them. It won't be happening again," Morrigan promised, reaching out to shake Clare's hand. Judging her to be in her mid-sixties, with fierce blue eyes and a gray braid that hung to her waist, Clare sized Morrigan up as someone she was happy to have on her side.

"It isn't your fault," Blake said, coming to stand by

Clare. "The Domnua are advancing. We'll need to move on immediately."

"I understand. It was an honor to fight on your behalf," Morrigan said, sweeping into a low bow in front of Clare. Startled, Clare grabbed her arm and pulled her up.

"Please don't bow to me. We're all fighting the same battle. I'm the same as you are," Clare said softly, the fine aftershocks of adrenaline making her voice shaky.

"Ah, 'tis kind of you, *Na Sirtheoir*, but no, we are not the same. It's I that should be thanking you. You're fighting for the world as we know it," Morrigan said kindly. "I'll get coffee on while you pack your things."

Morrigan slipped across the yard, and Clare turned to see Blake examining a wound in his arm.

"You're hurt," Clare pointed out, reaching out to touch his arm, but he pulled back from her. The slice didn't look deep, but its edges were tinged with silver.

"Don't touch it. It's one of their tricks. Once their poison is on you, they'll be able to track you more accurately."

"Poison!" Clare exclaimed.

Seamus had returned to the cottage and now came up to them, a small jar in his hand. Opening it, he dipped his fingers in a violet gel and smoothed it quickly over Blake's wound. The silver disappeared and the wound knit rapidly. Clare and Bianca looked at each other in disbelief.

"Well, now, we'd be billionaires if we could sell that healing salve," Bianca commented and Clare nodded.

"Isn't that the truth of it?"

"Enough talk. We must move. Don't even think we've won the battle. They were just testing our strength. You'll do well to remember this: While you battle for your world, they are battling for their freedom."

Which made them even more dangerous than Clare had initially assumed.

CHAPTER 24

They are fighting for their freedom.

Clare kept repeating the words in her head as they bumped along a narrow lane, Blake having chosen to take the back roads away from the farmhouse.

"Should I feel bad for the Domnua?" Clare finally asked, having worked her way around to what was bothering her.

Blake and Seamus both laughed at the same time.

"Not in the slightest, love. You'll do well to remember that they'll murder you without a second thought," Seamus said.

"Yeah, but, I mean, why? Like, is there any way we could all co-exist? You know how we feel about slavery and all." Clare shrugged, feeling a bit stupid but still wanting to know the answer.

"They've always been bad," Blake said, looking over at her. "They are of the dark underworld. Living on this plane of existence would not change their inherent darkness. It would only give them another playground."

"They're not like us, Clare," Seamus said. "They don't view right and wrong the way we do. There is no conscience. I suppose we'd call them sociopaths."

"I have a question," Bianca piped up, and Seamus slid his arm around her. Clare had noticed they pretty much hadn't stopped touching each other since the battle this morning, and she wondered what had transpired in the cottage during the night.

"How come they can be here? I mean, if Blake has been protecting Clare from them for years, and they seem to be able to just pop up out of nowhere and try to kill her – aren't they already free? Or here? What's stopping them?"

"Because the ones who come here to walk the earth are their army. Somehow, along the way, or woven into the curse, they were granted access."

"Well, then why wouldn't they just put their entire population into the army and come live on earth?" Bianca asked.

Silence filled the car for a moment.

"I have absolutely no idea. And isn't that a terrifying thought," Blake admitted. "Though now that it's been brought up I'll be sure to report it. We wouldn't want them to get ahead of themselves now, would we?"

"Is there a higher-up you're reporting to then?" Clare asked.

"Something like that," Blake said, then pressed his lips together.

Clare waited a moment, but no more information seemed to be forthcoming.

"I'm worried about my family," Clare said, moving on to the next topic that was circling in her too-busy brain. "I feel like I'll be leading danger right to their path."

"I've had them protected for a while," Blake said. "And I sent more when I knew we were coming this way. I just underestimated the protection we'd need on the way, is all."

"Is it good protection? Is it enough?" Clare asked, worry still kicking through her stomach. Judging by what she'd seen this morning, the Domnua were sneaky and they moved in packs.

"Aye, it's good. I promise no harm will come to your family," Blake said, reaching over to squeeze her hand softly. His touch reminded Clare of just where she'd been when she had been startled awake. Heat washed through her in both embarrassment and lust as she thought about sharing a bed with Blake.

"How much longer to your parents' home?" Bianca asked.

"Not far now."

"Will they be up? It's not quite full light," Bianca asked, and Clare looked to where the sun was just beginning to poke over the hills. Seeing the sun on a day in January was always considered a good thing.

"Up before dawn most days. They are farmers."

Nerves descended upon her as they drove toward Clifden. What would her parents think when she showed up on their doorstep at such an early hour with three friends in tow?

"Right here," Clare said, directing Blake away from the village and down a winding road. Soon, the sight of the village was hidden by hedges that grew wild and free along the side of the road.

"But a few moments more, up on the left," Clare instructed, and they all fell silent as Blake directed the car along a few more turns and then paused at a gravel driveway.

"This the one?"

"This is the one," Clare said softly, trying to see her childhood home through the eyes of her friends.

A ranch-style home, it was all one level with white stucco walls and simple brown trim. Her mother's window boxes weren't planted for the year, but in the summer, they would boast cheerful red blooms. Behind the house, a few outbuildings and a stable sat clustered together. Gently rolling green hills unfolded as far as the eye could see from there on.

"Is all this land your parents'?" Blake asked.

"Aye. They live simply, but they own a large tract of land," Clare said.

"It must have been lovely growing up here," Bianca said. She'd never been to Clare's home as they had rarely taken weekends away from the city.

Clare felt some of the tension in her stomach ease. "It

was fun to run the hills, I won't be denying that," she admitted.

"I can see how you ended up in geology. I mean aside from the obvious part regarding you being a Seeker and all that," Seamus said.

"Yes, plenty of land to dig in," Clare agreed as the car pulled to a stop. Her father, hearing the crunch of tires on the gravel, had poked his head from the barn.

"My dad," Clare said, pointing to her father. Wearing bib overalls, a canvas jacket, and a red knit cap, he pulled his gloves off and waved a hand as he moved toward the car.

Clare opened the door and hopped out.

"Dad!"

"Sure and that's a welcome surprise," Madden MacBride called out, laughing as he picked up speed across the yard. In moments, her face was buried in his neck, smelling the earthy scents of his aftershave and dirt, mixed together to make his own unique scent.

"I've missed you," Clare admitted.

"Why, it hasn't been that long since the holiday," Madden asked, his blue eyes searching hers. Caught for a moment in thought, Clare studied his ruddy face and light features.

"I've brought friends," Clare said, the thought still niggling at her brain, as her mum opened the front door of the house.

"Clare! Is something wrong?" Mary MacBride strode across the front yard, a plain blue apron tied over a long-sleeved jumper and khaki pants. Her blonde hair was just beginning to show gray and her blue eyes were alight with pleasure that held a hint of worry. Catching her in a hug, Mary pulled Clare tight.

Clare let herself be held for a moment as her mind whirled. Gently extricating herself from her mother's arms, she looked between both of her parents.

Why had she never seen this before?

"Will you introduce us to your friends?" Mary asked, looking over her shoulder at Blake, who had gotten out of the car. Clare watched him for a moment, and shook her head for him to stay back. Nodding, he slipped back into the car.

"Who is that man? Clare, what is going on?" Mary asked, running her hand down Clare's arm.

"Mum, why don't I look like either of you?"

Mary's hands dropped to her side as her eyes met Madden's.

Silence stretched between them as the moment drew out, the only sound coming from a sheep bleating in the barn.

Clare felt like her heart had jumped into her throat, and she tried to swallow as the moment stretched on seemingly forever.

"Clare, we need to talk."

She closed her eyes as the last remnants of the person she had known shattered in pieces around her.

CHAPTER 25

Though her world was rocked to the core, Clare waited quietly while her mother insisted on bringing everyone inside and serving them tea. When everyone was settled in the front room, Mary glanced at Madden.

"Clare, if we could speak to you in the other room?"

Clare knew her mother was trying to spare her any embarrassment or dramatics in front of her friends, but Mary wasn't the only one holding a secret. It didn't matter if her friends heard what Clare thought Mary was about to reveal.

"You can speak freely in front of them," Clare said, waving to where her friends sat huddled on a small settee and an armchair. The front room was her mother's favorite, and was covered in lace doilies and lace curtains, the walls crowded with prints and pictures. Clare's eyes fell on a picture of herself, not quite one year old, grinning like a cherub with fat auburn curls springing from her head.

She looked up to see that Blake had followed her eyes to the picture and then back to her. He smiled at her briefly, silently offering her his support. Clare gave him a small smile, dimly aware of his overt masculinity as his size made the lace-covered armchair look diminutive.

"I'm not sure…" Mary trailed off, wringing her hands. Madden stood stoically at her side, his arm wrapped around her.

"You're going to tell me that you're not my biological parents," Clare said, deciding to do the difficult part for them.

Mary gasped, bringing her hand to her mouth in a fist as tears welled in her pretty blue eyes.

"You knew."

"No, I didn't. A series of recent events has lead me to believe I might not be your child. But, no, I never knew. You are my mother, that's the truth of it," Clare said, crossing the room and wrapping her arms around her mother, who was now crying openly.

"You're our daughter and that's that," Madden said, nodding his head as though the matter was decided.

"Of course I am. Nobody can take that away from us," Clare assured him. She was too caught up in the grief on her mother's face to even try to deal with the tumult of emotions that swirled in her stomach.

"I'm so sorry I didn't tell you," Mary whispered and Clare reached out to wipe a tear from her cheek.

"I don't think you were meant to tell me," Clare said gently.

"Can you tell us how Clare came to be in your life?" Blake asked and Mary looked past Clare's shoulder.

"Ah well, sure and that's not of interest to all of you," Mary said, crossing her arms over her chest.

Clare glanced at Blake, then back to her suddenly nervous parents. Were they scared to reveal that there was magick involved?

"I know that I'm… special," Clare said, breaking the silence.

"We… we were struggling with having children, if ye ken," Madden said gruffly, his cheeks reddening with embarrassment at the subject matter.

"Of course, I understand," Clare said quickly, her arm still around her mother.

"And when she came to us, well, we couldn't turn our back on you, you see," Mary said, wiping the corner of her eye.

"Who was 'she'?" Blake asked.

"It was a rainy night in January," Mary said, then turned to look at Madden. "Maybe we should sit."

"I'll grab some whiskey," Madden said and Mary laughed, her first real smile since seeing them all arrive on her doorstep at such an early hour.

"It's a wee bit early for that, aren't you thinking?" Mary asked.

"Oh, right. More tea then," Madden said, and disappeared. Mary turned and addressed the room.

"He doesn't like to talk about that night. Makes him nervous," Mary said softly.

"Because of magick," Seamus said easily.

Mary started, her eyes going wide for a moment. "Ah, so it would seem," Mary said softly, slumping onto the arm of a chair.

Madden entered the room with two more steaming cups of tea and a small package tucked under his arm.

"Oh, dear, so it's time," Mary said, looking at the package under Madden's arm.

"Isn't that what she said? To give it to her when the time was right?" Madden asked.

"Yes, I suppose it is," Mary agreed, then blushed when she realized the younger people were all listening to them.

"Tell us about that night," Clare instructed, moving to sit across from them.

"We were in the stables with one of our dogs. She was pregnant, and we both wanted to sit with her while she went through her labor," Madden said, shrugging his shoulders. "You know, just because she was a stable dog doesn't mean she wasn't a good dog."

"You loved that dog," Mary agreed.

"Yes, well, we sat with her since we could tell her time was near. And the rain and wind had really picked up."

"But it was cozy there, you know, with the warm glow from the lights, and the dog was tucked up in a little nest of blankets on some hay. It was nice," Mary said, looking over at Madden fondly.

"It *was* nice. We were a bit nervous, but in a good mood. Excited for the puppies," Madden agreed.

"And then the dog began to growl," Mary remembered.

"Yes, that was it! The dog growling. At first we thought it was because she was in pain, but she was staring at the barn door."

"And then it blew wide open," Mary continued.

"And a woman stood there."

"I swear she was glowing." Their voices toppled over each other, the story that had been buried for so long now rushing to see the light of day.

"She was beautiful," Madden mused, and then patted Mary's leg. "Not as beautiful as my wife, that's for sure. But still, quite lovely."

"Oh, go on with yourself. She was stunning. In an ethereal way, you know? Just, almost lit from within really," Mary said, staring off into space for a moment before shaking her head. "She all but glided into the stable."

"Aye, it looked like she was floating, but maybe we were imagining it," Madden agreed.

"And her face, aye, it was pure kindness and joy. It wasn't until she was close that we realized she held a bundle in her arms," Mary said.

"Did she speak?" Bianca asked, her eyes the size of saucers.

"Aye, she said she was answering our prayers with a gift from her heart," Mary whispered, her eyes welling up as she looked over at Clare.

Clare felt her own eyes well up in response. There was no doubting the love her parents had for her.

"And she held out this tiniest of bundles," Madden said, holding his arms out in front of him as he remembered. "And we could just barely make out the teeniest face buried in the blankets."

"I started crying, straightaway," Mary said.

"Aye, she did. So I stood and walked to this woman and held my arms out for the bundle."

"I finally got a hold of myself and asked her who she was and where this baby came from," Mary said.

"What did she say?"

"She said her name was Danu and that you were a gift from the gods." Mary laughed a little and shook her head. "Which, you know, didn't really make sense because there's only one God."

Clare slid a glance at Blake and then back to her parents. They were both staunch Catholics and now would not be the time to get into a religious discussion with them.

"Maybe she did say God," Madden mused, the edges of the memory blurring with the years.

"Either way, I'm telling you, it was as if we were in the presence of an angel. And she handed me a package," Mary said, pointing her finger at the leather-wrapped package. "She told me to give this to you when you came asking us about what you are. And that was it."

"Where did she go?" Clare asked. Though her heart was pounding like crazy in her chest, she wanted to hear the rest of the story.

"Um, well." Madden's cheeks colored again.

"She blinked out of sight. It was just... she was there and then she wasn't. And we had a baby on our hands," Mary said, her eyes alight as she recalled the astonishment of that moment.

"It was quite a shock. I mean, we didn't have any formula, no breast milk, obviously, no baby supplies... really, just nothing."

"Madden left right on the spot and drove to the next town over to pick up some formula," Mary remembered with a smile. "And I held you the entire time. You looked at me for the longest time, and then closed your eyes and slept."

"What did you tell people then? About me?" Clare asked.

"Well, since you were such a teeny thing, we faked the pregnancy for the next few months," Mary said with a smile. "I put a pillow in my dress and stayed at the farm for the most part. It wasn't too long until I claimed I'd given birth, and your weight was more in line with a normal baby's weight by then. Everyone just accepted it and we went about our lives."

"And yet you knew I was magick," Clare said, watching both of their faces.

"I wouldn't call it magick, love. You were touched by an angel, is all. That makes you special," Madden said, a stubborn look on his face.

Clare glanced at Bianca, who just shrugged her shoulders. After considering for a moment, Clare decided to let the subject drop. What would the point be of arguing magick over religion? Arguing with someone rarely changed their beliefs. Ultimately, what mattered was that they had taken Clare in, given her a loving home, and allowed her to be exactly who she was. If they chose to believe she was a gift from the angels – so be it. She couldn't ask for anything more than that.

"Thank you for raising me," Clare said with a small smile.

"What happened to the dog?" Bianca asked, startling them all.

Madden slapped his knee and boomed with laughter.

"She had four healthy pups that very night. Great dogs. We kept them all, too. Felt they were special since they were there the night we got Clare."

"Can I see the package?" Clare asked, bringing their attention back to the package that lay on Madden's knee.

"Of course," Madden said, holding it up. Clare crossed the room to get it from him, but then bent and pressed her lips to his cheek and inhaled his scent again. "I love you."

"You too, my girl," Madden whispered in her ear.

"And you, as well, my sweet mother," Clare said, straightening and hugging her mother as well.

"Oh, I just… I have to say I feel like a weight's been lifted," Mary said, fanning her face and half laughing, half crying.

"Thank you for telling me," Clare said, clutching the package to her body and feeling the power radiating from it.

"Can you stay the night? I'll get breakfast on," Mary said.

Clare turned and raised an eyebrow at Blake, but he shook his head ever so slightly.

"We've got to keep moving. We can eat though," Clare said, looking at Blake and raising an eyebrow in question. He nodded slightly, and Clare smiled. Nothing made her mother happier than fixing a meal for a group of people.

"Perfect." Mary jumped up and clapped her hands, immediately bustling to the kitchen.

Madden stood. "I've got to finish my morning feeding. I'll be back in shortly."

"I'll help you with that," Blake said, and Clare looked at him in shock. What was he up to?

"That's great. It'll certainly make things go more quickly. Tell me, Blake, what do you do for work?" Madden asked as they stepped outside. Clare almost wished she could follow and listen in. Aside from being a Protector, what did Blake do with his time?

"Are you going to open the package?" Bianca hissed from where she still sat, her hands clutched in her lap.

"Oh! Right, the package," Clare said, shaking her head as she looked down at it.

Would it hold answers – or more questions?

CHAPTER 26

"*I* think I need a moment," Clare admitted as she sat down next to Bianca.

"Sure and that's a lot to process," Bianca said, reaching over and squeezing Clare's hand for a second. "I mean, you just learned you were pretty much adopted, your parents don't believe in magick, and now you have a gift from the Goddess Danu. That's quite a bit to take in."

Clare felt a laugh begin to bubble up her throat.

"I love you."

"You too. But you've got to hold it together. Let's see what we're dealing with here," Bianca said, nodding at the package.

"It's weird, right? Like a gift from a mother that I never knew?" Clare asked.

"Let's just hope it's something that aids you on your quest," Seamus said easily, his eyes alight with curiosity.

"It feels like it is. It's humming with power," Clare admitted, running her hands over the soft leather. She slowly unwrapped the leather cord that kept it closed, then unrolled the butter soft material until it lay flat against her legs. Inside was an item wrapped in tissue paper and a small card.

"Oh, it does look like a bit of a gift, doesn't it?" Bianca asked.

"Card or tissue first?" Clare murmured.

"Card first. It's only polite," Bianca said automatically, and Clare chuckled.

"Does it matter when the person gifting it to you isn't here to see you open it?"

"Well, I never thought about it like that."

"She is an all-knowing being," Seamus pointed out. "She certainly could be watching you."

"Better read the card first," Bianca and Clare said in unison.

Clare laughed as she picked up the card, then paused for a moment. It seemed like ever since she'd seen the silver-eyed musician in the pub, her life had been a series of moments that were forever changing her. This felt like another one of those moments. A small trickle of panic seized her stomach.

"What if it's bad? What if I can't come back from this knowledge?" Clare whispered.

"I think it's a little too late for that," Bianca said.

Clare nodded, her thumb under the slit of the gold envelope. Taking a breath, she slid the flap open. Inside, a card was tucked away. Clare gently pulled the card free, not wanting to harm the paper.

"Love is the light that shines its truth in darkness," she read aloud.

Clare looked up at Bianca.

"That's it?" Bianca asked.

"That's it," Clare said, oddly disappointed. She wasn't sure what she had been expecting but she felt a little let down.

"It's another clue!" Seamus said, excitement radiating from him as he got up and bounced around the room.

"Sure and you don't think this is a clue?" Clare asked.

"It is! It has similar language, doesn't it? Truth, light, all of that... you know what we're looking for is the truth-stone, right? So now we've just got to figure out the riddle," Seamus said, a wide smile splitting his face.

"All fun and games until the Domnua get us," Bianca agreed.

Clare began to unwrap the tissue paper, the hum of power a seductive caress upon her skin. She gasped when she saw what lay inside.

"Why, it's positively lovely, isn't it? Right shiny too," Bianca marveled.

An intricate gold ring, delicate vines weaving together to hold a beautifully cut aquamarine, lay on the paper. The stone, the purest of ocean blues, seemed to glow from within.

"It's stunning," Clare breathed, gently picking it up.

"Do you think it will fit?" Bianca asked.

Clare slid the ring on the ring finger of her right hand. It seemed to morph and meld to her skin, becoming one with her instantly. The power she felt from it seemed to hum up her arm and then settle in her core, having found its home.

"I think it just transferred power to me or something," Clare whispered, staring in awe down at the ring.

"Good, we need all the help we can get," Seamus said.

"Breakfast is on," Mary called from the kitchen, startling them away from thoughts of magick powers and ancient quests.

"There'll be time for this," Bianca said, patting Clare on her arm as she stood. "For now, let's make your mother happy and enjoy a good home-cooked breakfast."

And so Clare tucked the card in her back pocket, the ring humming on her hand, and went to make her mother happy.

CHAPTER 27

*I*t was mid-morning by the time they left the farm, Clare hugging her parents extra-long on the way out with a promise to stay in touch. Neither of them had asked for more details on what had prompted Clare's visit, and Clare hadn't elaborated.

Sometimes, ignorance really was bliss.

Or in this case, a restful mind so her parents didn't worry too much.

Clare ran her finger over the ring, watching the play of light on the stone, as she thought over her morning. Sure, it had been filled with some pretty deep revelations about who and what she was. But the simple pleasures of life – eating food cooked with love around a table full of people you love – reminded her of just what was important to her. And if having to conquer the Domnua and find the Stone of Destiny meant keeping those she loved safe, well, it was no question what she would do.

Clare slid a glance over to where Blake drummed his fingers on the steering wheel in time to the rock music that pumped from the speakers. She'd seen a different side of him today – one that had both surprised her and charmed her at the same time. Peeking out the window from time to time had given her glimpses of him working side-by-side with her father as they went about the morning chores that every farm had. At one point, her father had said something that made Blake throw his head back and laugh, and Clare hadn't been able to stop herself from smiling at the picture he made.

Then he'd gone and sealed his place in her mother's heart by helping her set the table and revealing his grandmother's soda bread recipe – on penalty of death if she ever shared it with another soul.

Clare hadn't missed the look her mother had given her.

He's a keeper.

It wasn't looking like she was going to get out of this quest with her heart intact, Clare mused as she twisted the ring on her finger and considered the power she felt pulsing from it. What was Danu trying to teach her? And where should they go to next?

"Where are you taking us?" Clare asked.

Blake reached over and turned the volume on the radio down a few notches.

"Wherever the wind may blow, pretty one," Blake said.

Clare looked out the window and bit her lip to hold back a smile. She needed to remember that he was the one who had requested they keep their distance from each other.

"Your parents are nice," Seamus said from the back.

Clare turned and smiled at him.

"Aren't they? Just really good people. I had a lovely upbringing with them. Frankly, I don't care that they didn't give birth to me – they are my parents through and through."

"Absolutely. You can see it in their love for you. It just shines right through," Bianca agreed and Clare smiled at her too.

"And we've got another clue and you have more power," Seamus exclaimed, bringing his fingers to his chin and stroking thoughtfully. "I wonder what kind of power it is."

"Maybe it makes my freeze thing last longer?" Clare said, still feeling mildly uncomfortable about this power she held. Less than a week ago her biggest concern was gathering more research for her dissertation. Now she was considering her powers and trying to save the world.

Not a typical day.

"You're about to find out," Blake said, his voice sharp.

Clare had a moment of sheer panic as he jerked the steering wheel to the right and sent them bouncing off the road into the field next to it. Clare's head almost hit the roof as they careened over another grassy knoll and Blake picked up speed.

"What's happening?" Clare gasped, turning to look back at the road.

"Domnua," Blake bit out, his eyes focused on the uneven terrain ahead of them. Bianca screamed as Seamus rolled down the window and slid out until half his body was hanging outside of the SUV.

Clare blinked her eyes, afraid for a moment that she was just seeing things, but then gasped as a wall of silver seemed to streak across the land, like a dust storm being blown by angry fairy winds, closing in on the SUV.

Seamus, a bow and arrow mysteriously in his hand, shot arrow after violet arrow into the cloud of Domnua, but it was evident that his arrows could only do so much.

"Drive faster," Bianca screeched; Blake didn't turn his head from the path in front of him.

A trickle of sweat slid down Clare's back as panic threatened to overtake her. It was then that the ring pulsed against her palm, reminding her of the power that lay within her.

"Hang on, Seamus, I'm coming," Clare screeched. Unbuckling her seatbelt, she clambered into the back seat, and then over one more seat until she sat on top of the luggage in the back and stared directly out the back window.

"Does this window open?" Clare yelled, unsure if her magick would ricochet off glass. A more seasoned practitioner might have known the answer to that question, but Clare was only a few days into this whole fae-seeker gig.

Amazingly, the window slid down and a cool breeze blasted Clare in the face. Kneeling, she braced her left hand on the side of the car and leaned out, holding her right hand in front of her. For a moment, the world seemed to still as panic clawed at her throat. The car was racing across uneven terrain and a thousand Domnua were charging after them, moving faster than any car could go. And she was supposed to do something about it? Glancing back, she caught Bianca's terrified expression.

"Get 'em, Clare!" Bianca yelled, putting on a brave face.

Clare turned back around to face the storm. Reaching deep into her mind, she focused on the ball of power that formed in her core and, pulling it up, she unraveled it until it shot out from her hand like a whip cracking. There was no light, no theatrics, nothing – and for a second, Clare thought her power hadn't worked.

Then the storm disappeared.

"Holy hell," Seamus shouted.

Two Domnua riders remained, though they had slowed in their approach. Perched high atop silvery steeds, they glowed far brighter than the cloud of Domnua that had been surrounding them.

"Must be the generals," Seamus shouted, raising his bow.

In a flash, they too had disappeared, leaving nothing but a rolling green field and the beginning of winter rain in their midst. The droplets fell in flat plops, hitting the silvery puddles that lay splattered amidst the grass, the earth seeming to reach up and swallow its own.

"What the hell just happened?" Blake called back to them, his speed still bordering on terrifying.

Clare eased herself back into the car, allowing herself to fall back onto the luggage for a moment and look up at the ceiling of the car as they bumped along. Her heart hammered in her chest as she tried to comprehend what had just happened. The ring on her hand still glowed with an almost ethereal light; its heat trailed up her arm and coursed through her very core.

If this was the one gift she could have from her biological mother, well, it had proved to be a worthy one.

"Clare!" Bianca popped her head over the back of the seat so Clare was now looking at her best friend's upside down face.

"Bianca," Clare said evenly, still trying to catch her breath.

"Tell me you didn't just go and level an entire army of Domnua in one fell swoop," Bianca said, her eyes alight with excitement.

"It seems that perhaps I did indeed," Clare managed to say before Bianca squealed and planted a series of kisses on her forehead and cheeks.

"It's better than having Wonder Woman as a bestie, I tell you," Bianca crowed, pulling herself back over the seat.

Seamus popped his head over to look down at her.

"Sure and that was quite brilliant, if I do have to say. Far more effective than my bow and arrow," Seamus said cheerfully, but his eyes were shrewd. "Sure you're doing all right then?"

"I'm just processing what happened."

"I'm thinking Blake's a wee bit worried, so if you wouldn't mind popping up and reassuring him…" Seamus said gently, and Clare nodded.

Sitting up, Clare turned so she could see the front of the car. Blake's eyes met hers in the mirror, the startling blue of his gaze seeming to burn through her as he assessed her in the rearview mirror.

"I'm fine," Clare called.

"That's fine, then. I'm still going to get us to a safe place," Blake said evenly, not reducing the car's speed. Clare did catch a relieved look pass across his face before she lay back down on the luggage and wondered what he meant by a safe place.

And tried not to crow over the fact that she'd just leveled an entire army with one puff of magick from her hands. One thing she'd learned in life already was that getting cocky always led to downfall. Clare held up her hand and studied the ring again, reminding herself just where that flash of power had truly come from.

It was always best to remain humble.

CHAPTER 28

*B*lake kept his eyes on the field ahead of them, doing his best to dodge any major dips and potholes. He scanned constantly, reaching out with his senses to see if any other Domnua were about to spring an attack.

Though his eyes were on the landscape ahead of him, his heart was in the cargo with Clare. He wasn't entirely sure if he would ever forget seeing her hanging out of the back of his car while a thousand Domnua streaked like the hounds of hell across the hills.

Blake wasn't sure exactly when he'd fallen for Clare.

Part of him thought it might have been in the first instant he saw her, tentatively exploring the Trinity campus, her wild curls whipping around her head in the wind. Or perhaps it had been when he'd finally tasted her – the very essence of her searing its way straight to his core.

Seeing her with her parents – being both quick to

protect them and, at the same time, vulnerable with them – had opened his eyes to a new aspect of her. And when he'd finally decided he'd seen all sides of Clare, she'd all but thrown herself out of his car to protect them from evil.

Yeah, it was hard to not love a woman like that.

It was his destiny to protect her, his goddess-given duty to assist her on her path, and only when she had fulfilled her own destiny would he be free to truly love her.

And hopefully, when that time came, she'd love him right back. Because there was one thing Blake was certain about.

He would die without her in his life.

For Clare, finding the stone was her destiny.

For him? Clare was his.

CHAPTER 29

"Where are you taking us then? Where is this safe space? How do you know it's safe?" Bianca asked as they tore along the road. Blake had deemed it safe to get back on the gravel path and they now proceeded at a breakneck pace to whatever destination Blake had decided upon.

"We'll be there shortly," Blake said and turned the music back up.

Clare sat up and peered over the seat at Bianca, who turned and rolled her eyes at Clare. Slapping her hand over her mouth, she pushed down a giggle. It felt a lot like a father telling his children to stop asking 'are we there yet?'

But in this moment they did feel like a family, Clare thought as she smiled at her friend. Bianca's cheek held a smudge of dirt and Seamus's hair stood on end. They were all unshowered, a bit rough around the edges, and far more serious about their mission than they had been yesterday.

There was nothing like having your lives on the line to put the seriousness of the situation in perspective, Clare thought as she looked down at the aquamarine ring again.

Clare glanced up as the car turned right, bumping off of the gravel road onto an uneven dirt lane that wound its way up a hill. The hedges grew tall, surrounding the path, and blocking the view.

"What if someone is driving from the other direction?" Clare asked Blake.

"You crack the window and listen," Blake said, having turned the music off and rolled his window down. They proceeded down the lane at a snail's pace, twisting and turning before finally cresting over one last hill.

"Oh!" Clare exclaimed, and blinked. She hadn't been expecting this.

A large home, reminiscent of an old castle, sat proudly on a ledge, the hill at its back, the world unrolling beneath its glorious green hills. Even on this gray day, Clare could imagine waking up here every morning and drinking tea while looking over the surrounding fields.

Dark gray stone wound up to a turret, and paned glass lined all the windows, with rooms sticking out in all directions from the main two-story section. It looked like it had been added on to over the years, and the house was hodgepodge mix of old and new.

"Is this... a castle or something?" Bianca asked.

"The turret and the great hall were once part of a castle. The rest of the castle crumbled to the ground. My grandfather decided to save the turret and the great hall, and then built rooms onto it to make it a house."

Clare swallowed past a lump in her throat.

"Your grandparents. This is your family home?"

"Aye, though it's just my grandmother now."

"What about your parents?" Bianca asked, as the car rolled to a stop by two wooden doors that formed an arch.

"Dead," Blake bit out and the car went silent.

One side of the arched door opened and a tiny woman, whose head barely reached above the handle of the door, poked her head out. Seeing the car, a joyous smile split her lined face. White hair was braided into a bun at the nape of her neck, and she wore a pretty red paisley apron over a bright turquoise blouse and a striped skirt that reached her calves.

"She looks like a doll," Bianca breathed.

Blake shot her a look over his shoulder.

"Her name's Esther. And she's my favorite person in the world."

"I can see why," Bianca agreed and opened the door. Clare sat where she was and watched as Blake rounded the car and snatched his grandmother up, twirling her in a big hug while she laughed and hugged him back. Clare's heart seemed to sigh a little as she watched them.

"I know," Bianca said, opening the back of the SUV and looking in at Clare. "It's enough to make your ovaries sit up and beg."

Clare snorted, shaking her head at her friend as she climbed over the luggage and snagged her bag on the way.

Looking around, she could just make out the thin line of magick that surrounded this place. Of course Blake had protected his grandmother.

Just like he'd protected her parents.

Clare shot a look over her shoulder at where Esther smiled up at Blake, her heart in her eyes, and tried to remain unaffected. He'd asked her to keep her distance, hadn't he?

"He's warded the place," Clare said to Seamus as he rounded the back of the car and grabbed some of the bags.

"How can you tell?" Bianca demanded, immediately turning to shield her hand over her eyes as she searched the landscape.

"It's just a faint shimmer that I can see across the way," Clare shrugged and pointed. "Over there, and there, and – well, it looks like at all the cardinal points."

"She's right," Blake said, coming up to them and making Clare jump. Whenever he was close to her, it was as if she felt a magnetic pull. Forcing herself to ignore it, Clare met his eyes.

"I'm starting to be able to pick up on more magickal things, I think."

"That's good. It will aid you on your quest. Now, if you'd like to meet my grandmother? We're safe to stay here for the night."

"No longer though?"

"I'd prefer not to draw too many Domnua here to test the strength of my wards," Blake said simply, throwing the strap of a bag over his shoulder and automatically taking

Clare's bag too. Clare wanted to struggle with the strap for a moment, but then allowed him to take it. Some battles were not worth fighting.

Clare followed Blake to where his grandmother stood, a beaming half-pint of a woman, and felt nerves suddenly assault her stomach.

"You must be Clare. A pleasure to finally meet you," Esther said, reaching up with both of her arms open. Clare automatically bent and hugged her – it was hard to resist such an outpouring of genuine kindness.

"Nice to meet you. It sounds like you've heard about me, but I'm sorry to say that I haven't heard anything about you," Clare said, smiling down into eyes the same sea blue as Blake's. "I look forward to rectifying that on our visit."

Esther chuckled and squeezed Clare's arm.

"You weren't supposed to know about us until it was time. Now, it is time. So, I welcome you and your friends to my home and I hope that you'll find peace here while you stay."

She followed Esther into the great hall and her mouth dropped open. The room opened up into an expanse of tall windows, a three-story fireplace, and huge dark beams that crisscrossed the ceiling. The massive fireplace, made of thick blocks of multi-colored stone, housed a fire that could easily roast an entire boar. Next to the fireplace was an Esther-sized doorway that Clare presumed led to the turret.

In front of the fireplace, a huge faded red oriental-style

rug lay, and worn leather couches and chairs were arranged into small conversation corners. In the middle, a long table with easily sixteen chairs held tea service and enough baked goods to feed a small army.

"You baked!" Blake said, his eyes alight with pleasure as he looked back at the rest of them. "You're in for a real treat when Grandmother bakes."

"No food until you wash up. Blake, show everyone to their rooms," Esther said with a smile. Clare could feel the happiness at having company radiating from Esther's very being, and a part of her just wanted to curl up on the couch by the fire and talk to Esther for days.

They followed Blake across the great hall to where it narrowed into a hallway that split up into three parts. Taking the left turn, they passed a series of doors until the hallway ended at two doors.

"Seamus, Bianca, your two rooms," Blake said, gesturing to the two doors. Clare caught Bianca's quick flush as she glanced at Seamus and then pushed her door open. Neither made a comment on the close proximity of their bedrooms, but Clare had a pretty good idea what they were thinking about.

"We're on the other end – where the hall forked right," Blake said, backing up and taking Clare's arm. All of her senses seemed to spring alive at his touch and she walked with him silently as he led her back to the main hallway and down another winding corridor until the hall ended – at a single door.

Clare raised an eyebrow and turned to look up at him.

His nearness to her was frying the circuits in her brain a bit, but she held strong as she narrowed her eyes at him.

"A little presumptuous, isn't it?"

A wicked grin flashed across Blake's face before he pushed the door open.

"Two bedrooms. A connecting living area in the middle," Blake said, allowing Clare to brush past him and into the room.

He was right, Clare fumed to herself, as she studied the room she had stepped into. With low ceilings, a warm golden wood floor, and a small couch and armchair, it was the perfect cozy nook to curl up and read a book in. And on either side of the room, arched doorways stood open.

"I'll take this one," Clare decided, moving to the right door.

"Your wish is my command," Blake teased.

Clare rolled her eyes, though a decidedly naughty wish slid through her mind for an instant. Clare pushed the arched door wide and gasped at the pretty room that greeted her. A large bed with an intricate wrought-iron headboard dominated the room, with a pretty spring-green coverlet lying over crisp white linens. Delicate lace curtains framed the windows and two dark wooden built-in bookcases lined both walls.

"The toilet," Blake said, pointing to a door to her right. She pushed it open to see a large tub – big enough for two – and gleaming modern amenities.

"I'm surprised. This is one of the nicest bathrooms I've ever seen," Clare admitted in astonishment.

"Because they spent so much time up here, isolated from the world, they figured they might as well have the best of everything," Blake agreed, stepping out and back into the small connecting room. Moments later, he returned and put her bag on the bed.

"Will we have time to freshen up before tea?" Clare asked, looking down at her rumpled appearance.

"Maybe just a splash of water on the face? Grandmother is eager for guests and I'd like to take a walk before it gets dark."

Clare nodded, resigning herself to holding off on washing up until later. She promised herself a lazy soak in the tub later tonight, once the house quieted down and everyone succumbed to sleep.

Making quick use of the bathroom, Clare did splash some water on her face, and quickly braided the mess of her hair back from her face. A swift change into jeans and a gray jumper, and she met Blake back in the main room.

"Where does Esther sleep?" Clare asked as they headed back down the hallway. She noticed he had to duck to make it through the doorway. He'd also changed, this time into a green flannel shirt that he'd rolled to his muscular forearms.

"Her room and the kitchen are down the main hallway, as well as a crafting room, a canning room, and a study."

"Wow, this place is a real hodgepodge," Clare said, following him out as the hall widened into the great hall again. Esther sat on a leather chair by the fire, chatting animatedly with Seamus. Bianca hovered near the tea and Clare knew her friend was eyeing up the scones.

"Ah, there they are," Esther called, her voice echoing across the hall.

"Sorry if we kept you waiting," Clare said as she neared. "I also apologize for dropping in on you without notice. Though it seems you were prepared?" She wondered when Blake had had time to alert her that they were coming.

"Aye, 'tis no worry. I knew you were on your way," Esther said easily, rising and crossing to the table. "Sit, sit and eat. I've got a roast of lamb in cooking for later tonight too."

Bianca groaned and rubbed her stomach. "I'll be putting on a stone by the time I leave here, I will."

"Sure and you'll work it off fighting some Domnua," Esther said with a laugh and Clare glanced sharply at her. Who was this woman, that she so easily spoke of the Domnua?

Esther met her gaze. "There'll be time for questions. First, though – tea."

Tea, always a constant, Clare mused as she sat and poured herself a cup of tea. Carefully considering the pile of baked goods in front of her, Clare selected a cinnamon scone and an oversized blueberry muffin with sugar crumbles on top.

"Grandmother's a seer," Blake said, sitting next to Clare and biting into a biscuit. Clare started, then met Esther's eyes across the table.

"That's the truth of it, then," Esther admitted easily.

Bianca's eyes went wide for a moment, the scone pausing on the way to her mouth, before she let loose with a barrage of questions. Tuning out her friend as she peppered Esther with questions, Clare looked at Blake.

"That's how she knew we were coming. And knows what I am," she said quietly.

"Aye, she's known about you for a long time. I couldn't hide what I was from her. It was a great honor to our family that I was selected as a Protector," Blake said, finishing off a biscuit and reaching for a scone.

"It's strange to me… that so many people knew more about me than I did," Clare admitted. Esther, catching her words, smiled across the table at her.

"Child, there are things in life you don't need to know until it's the proper time – that it will unfold as it should."

"But how can you trust that? I mean, doesn't it make you feel out of control to just… leave everything to fate?" Clare countered.

Esther's smile deepened. "True, 'tis easier for me because I'm a seer. But there's no point in being upset about what you didn't once know. It doesn't change where you sit now. Look forward, child, look forward," Esther said.

A roll of thunder, soft in the distance, interrupted their conversation. Blake stood, pushing back his chair and looking pointedly at Clare.

"I'm going to take Clare for a walk on the grounds. Will you keep Esther company?"

"We will. I have a million questions for her. Most importantly, her recipe for these scones," Bianca gushed.

Clare stood, abandoning the rest of her tea to see what Blake wanted to show her. She followed him to where he stood by the two arched doors, her coat already in his hand, his eyes steady on hers.

"Don't you think that was a bit rude?" Clare asked as she took the coat and stepped outside. In the distance, a storm brewed on the horizon, its thick clouds swirling high into the sky. Thunderstorms like this were rare in Ireland, and Clare wondered if there was magick behind it.

"It's fine. She loves me. Plus, we'll be back shortly, since this storm will be here in but a moment," Blake said. Surprising Clare, he reached out and took her hand. Heat, and the hum of power, radiated up her palm and through her whole body, making her suddenly fiercely and intensely aware of his nearness.

Clare schooled her breath as they hiked around the side of the house and climbed higher onto the hill behind it, Clare falling into an even pace next to Blake.

"How did your parents die?" Clare asked, then immediately felt bad for breaking their companionable silence with such a difficult question.

"They were killed protecting me a month after I was born," Blake said. "The Domnua realized I had been marked as a Protector. They were trying to get to me. My parents saved my life."

The ultimate blood sacrifice, Clare thought dully, as she tried to imagine growing up without her parents.

. "I'm sorry," Clare said. What else can you say to someone who had experienced such a loss?

"I had my grandparents, so it wasn't all bad. But, well, my father didn't believe. He refused to see what I was and he didn't protect our little family. They should have brought me here right away, as soon as they knew what I was. But they didn't. And they lost their lives for not believing," Blake said, his tone even as they crested the top of the hill. In the exact middle sat a circle of stones, one stone slightly taller and giving the appearance of an altar.

Blake led her to the circle and sat down on a stone, patting the space next to him. She sat down and leaned into his warmth, not entirely surprised when his arm came around her. Together, they sat in silence for a moment as they looked across the hills of Ireland, their view unobstructed for miles.

"You're trying to tell me to suspend all disbelief or I might get killed," Clare finally said. Blake sighed, squeezing her shoulder a bit. She wanted to nestle into his warmth more, but restrained herself.

"I'm saying that you have to trust your destiny. Our paths all weave together, in and out, forming the tapestry of this world and into the next. You pull one string and the entire tapestry can unravel. I'm asking you to suspend your disbelief, push that science mind down, and believe in the unbelievable. Look," Blake pointed.

Clare squinted at the horizon. "The storm?"

"Beneath the storm," Blake said softly.

Clare narrowed her eyes at the place where the storm clouds crept along the hills, seeming to devour the green within the grey mists, and then her eyes widened. Beneath the rolling clouds were streaks of silver – and not from lightning bolts.

"The Domnua are bringing the storm," Clare breathed.

Blake pulled her even more tightly against him. "Aye, they bring the storm," Blake agreed.

"But, but – what are we going to do? We need to prepare! We have to fight," Clare gasped, feeling panic rise in her as she thought about the diminutive Esther, feeding her friends scones by a hot fire.

"We're protected here," Blake said, reaching over to put his hand to her face and turning her chin so that she looked up at him. "This circle we sit upon is one of the most powerful in all of Ireland. And you know why?"

"No, I don't," Clare said, lost in his eyes as the storm raged behind her.

Within her.

"Love," Blake said, brushing his lips against hers in a gentle hint of a kiss, the promise of his heat anything but gentle.

"I don't understand," Clare gasped against his mouth.

"Love centers these stones. Thousands of years of love, births, deaths, marriages, marriage proposals, circle in and out upon these stones. A kiss is anything but a kiss and everything more than a kiss while sitting here," Blake murmured, and then took her lips again, pulling her under, seducing her with his touch – capturing her heart with his words.

And as the storm built behind them, all Clare could hear was the singing of her heart and the truth that lay hidden there.

CHAPTER 30

*H*ours later, they sat at dinner while the storm raged outside, the wind howling with the angry cries of the Domnua held at bay by the wards.

Clare found herself blushing as she looked at Blake from the corner of her eyes. She felt weird and raw, almost like he'd opened a wound when he'd kissed her in the circle of stones. Why had he taken her there? And kissed her like that in that exact spot? After he'd specifically told her to give him space. Clare felt like she was being drawn slowly into Blake's web – and a more willing victim she'd never known.

She speared a piece of potato, coated in a dill and brown butter sauce. Esther had outdone herself with the meal, and they all relaxed around the table, the fire crackling away, a lovely red wine in their glasses.

Clare looked around at these people, whom she cared

very deeply about – even Esther, though she'd just met her today. The heart recognized its own.

The conversation lulled as everyone fell into a rare moment of contented silence. Except for Clare – she was silent, but anxious. Nerves ranged through her body and she felt like a live wire that was about to zap anyone who touched it. She couldn't decide if it was her nervousness over hearing the cries of the Domnua surrounding them, or if it was because every time she looked at Blake, her stomach seemed to flip itself over.

"Now that we've been fed and are settled down, I have something to say," Esther said, her voice carrying surprisingly well in such a large room. Clare wondered how the acoustics worked in such a space, but imagined they'd taken that into consideration hundreds of years ago when it was built.

"I'm always delighted to listen to your words of wisdom," Blake winked at his grandmother and Clare felt that funny little flip low in her stomach again. Seeing Blake with his guard down around his grandmother was enough to make any woman swoon.

"It may come as a surprise to you," Esther continued with a smile for her grandson, "but Blake was not the first Protector we've had in this family. Which is highly unusual, actually."

Blake nodded at her. This was no news to him, it seemed, but Clare was very interested.

"Who else was a Protector?" Bianca asked.

Esther's smile grew wider. "His grandfather. My husband."

Clare's mouth dropped open. "Does that mean you're *Na Sirtheoir*?

"I am, indeed, I am. Or I was, I should say. Retired."

"But... but you lived," Clare gasped. "You're alive to tell the tale. You didn't find it and yet, here you are."

Esther beamed at her across the table and lifted her glass of wine in a silent toast. "To seek does not always mean to find what you thought you were looking for. Sometimes it is only to gather more information along the way. I wasn't meant to find the treasure, only to bring us closer to finding it."

"So every generation that didn't find it, helped gather more clues? It all culminates with me?" Clare's voice rose on the last word as panic resumed its stealthy dance in her core.

"Not just you, child. Never just you. All of us fighting for the light. We're all responsible for the outcome of whatever may happen. You're just the first of four to finish this round. Have faith. I do," Esther said, her eyes no longer beaming, but coolly sizing Clare up.

"How can you have faith? You don't even know me," Clare asked, her voice cracking again. She liked Esther. The last thing she wanted to do was to let her down. Or... everyone, really.

"I can see. It's one of my gifts, child. As a seer, I can see your soul – your very essence. You've only to look within to see the light. Remember that, you've only to look within. You'll find your answers there," Esther said, her gaze locked on Clare's. For a moment, a tangible thread of power seemed to race between them until Clare nodded in understanding. She'd been given a gift here tonight. One that she would need to use when the time called for it.

"I also have something for you," Esther continued, and patting Blake on the arm, she pointed to a small box sitting next to the fireplace. "Blake, be a love and get that box for me."

"Do all Protectors end up in love with the Seekers?" Bianca burst out. Clare could have banged her forehead against her dinner plate.

"Not all, no," Esther twinkled at Bianca. "But the lucky ones do."

Clare's cheeks burned. She refused to look at Blake, though she was aware of him with every last ounce of her being.

"And Grandfather certainly was the lucky one, to have won such a beautiful rose as yourself," Blake said as he returned to the table and placed the box next to Esther's plate.

Helpless not to look up at Blake, Clare's eyes locked with his and fire screamed its way through her. There was no denying the truth of it – she wanted this man with every breath she took. Whether it was because of their magickal connection, their mental attraction, or just good old-fashioned lust, Clare was ready to cry uncle.

One corner of Blake's mouth quirked up and he

seemed to read her decision. Blushing, Clare looked down and then took a sip of her wine to cool her throat.

"This is for you," Esther said, passing over the wooden box, its cover inlaid with intricate Celtic designs.

"Another clue," Bianca breathed. Seamus nudged her with his shoulder to shush her.

"It's truly lovely," Clare murmured, brushing her hands over the wood, the corners smooth from age, and lifted the cover open. Inside lay a necklace on a velvet-lined interior, along with a small dagger and a rolled piece of paper.

"What is it?" Bianca demanded, craning to see over the top of the box.

Clare laughed, tilting the box so she could see. "It's a lovely aquamarine necklace, with the mark of the *Na Sirtheoir* in the middle. It's really quite stunning," Clare said, lifting the heavy gold chain from the box and holding it aloft. A ripple of power hummed from it and seemed to connect to the stone on her finger.

"Were these once a pair?" Clare asked, holding her hand up for Esther to see.

"Aye, they were. I was delighted to see you had it with you. We've been unable to track it for years now," Esther said, her face a beacon of joy.

"It's been charmed then. I'll be stronger for wearing it?" Clare asked, slipping the necklace over her head. It hung heavily against her neck, the aquamarine nestled between her breasts just below the smaller pendant that Branna had given her.

"You'll be stronger for the wearing of it," Esther confirmed.

"And the dagger?" Seamus asked, unable to withhold his curiosity either. Clare reached into the box and pulled out the small dagger, no longer than the length of her hand, with a heavily carved handle that curved toward the *Na Sirtheoir* mark at the base of the hilt. The blade gleamed in the light, no speck of corrosion marring its beautiful surface.

"Use it when the time is right," Esther said softly, "Keep it with you at all times. If you freeze and forget your magick, remember that this dagger will always help you."

Clare nodded, the nerves tripping her up again as she considered having to use the dagger in a hand-to-hand fight. Against whom? Or what?

All questions for another time, she decided, as she reached for the roll of paper. Not a night by the fire with good food and good friends.

Carefully, Clare unrolled the paper, glancing up at Blake quickly before looking down at the words written there.

"They're Gaelic. I'm sorry, I'm not the best at remembering my Irish," Clare admitted and turned the paper so that everyone else could see.

"Ah," Esther said and the table quieted.

"The saint walks his path in darkness."

CHAPTER 31

They'd spent at least another hour on the couches by the fire while they debated the meaning of the clue. Finally, Clare had admitted it was time for sleep. Between the rude awakening in the early hours of the morning and the constant level of stress they were under, she was ready for one night of rest.

Before she faced whatever cryptic message the clue held for her.

Clare sat on the edge of the tub, knowing it was foolish to indulge herself this way, but Esther had told her that she'd left lavender bath soap for her by the tub when she'd bent to kiss her goodnight. It was her way of telling Clare to take the moments – the small, seemingly mundane in-between moments in life – and to cherish those times too.

And even if it kept her up another twenty minutes or so, Clare would wager she'd sleep like a baby after a nice soak.

Unwrapping the soft white towel she had wound around herself, Clare slid into the fragrant water, the soapy bubbles enveloping her in their warmth and heavenly scent. She let out a small whimper of pleasure as water caressed her skin, easing the aches of a long few days. Leaning her head back against the rim of the huge tub, Clare closed her eyes and let her mind drift.

And when her thoughts landed solidly on Blake, she didn't stop herself from examining her feelings for him.

It was more than just his touch, though his kisses – hell, his very presence – ignited every nerve ending in her body until she was in a state of hyperawareness. But it was the instant connection she'd felt with him – the one that had made her push him away and go toe-to-toe with him despite how much she wanted to pull him closer – that resonated with her.

She could spend her days going toe-to-toe with him and then making up in the bedroom in the nights, Clare thought, as lust slipped low in her belly. She knew that now wasn't the time for it – what with the fate of the world in their hands – but damn if she didn't want to sneak into his room and slide beneath his covers.

Not that she'd ever be bold enough to do that.

But it was fun to think about.

"Clare?"

A gentle knock on her bedroom door made her jump. She hadn't closed the bathroom door, but she couldn't see the door from where she sat in the tub.

"Um, yes?" Clare called, closing her eyes in embarrassment.

Clare heard the slight squeak of the door hinges as the door pushed open, then silence. Finally Blake cleared his throat.

"Esther sent me to bring you a cup of tea. She said it'll help you sleep without dreams." Blake's voice carried to her from the room, and Clare kept her eyes closed as she debated either inviting him to join her or just dying on the spot.

"Thank you," Clare called, her voice cracking.

"Is everything all right then?" Blake asked, his voice nearer now and Clare squeezed her eyes shut.

"Aye, 'tis fine," Clare said, her voice breathless as a shiver of excitement worked its way through her.

"I can see that," Blake said softly from the doorway.

Clare opened her eyes slowly to see him standing there in loose sweatpants and a t-shirt, holding a cheerful blue mug with daisies on it. His eyes held hers for one interminably long second.

Clare's mouth went dry, as her eyes held his, and the moment stretched between them. Blake moved first, coming to sit at the edge of the tub, as he placed the cup of tea by her head.

"Thanks," Clare said softly, and Blake only nodded, his eyes never leaving hers.

"Tell me to go," Blake said, his voice but a scratch in the darkness.

"I can't," Clare whispered, desperate with need.

"It hurts to breathe," Blake said, bringing his fist to his chest right beneath his heart. "Right here, it hurts to breathe. Every second that I'm near you, that I can't touch you – that I don't know you're mine. It's a constant pain that's never gone away. I've ached for you since the moment I set eyes on you."

His heart, laid bare at the edge of the tub, and Clare had only to pick it up or let him bleed.

"You told me to give you space," Clare said, her tone accusatory. "You pushed me away."

"I had to. I can't sacrifice everything. But now I know the only thing I'm sacrificing is the joy of being with you, beside you, within you. I'm asking you to share yourself with me. All of you," Blake whispered, his eyes gleaming in the light that spilled into the bathroom from the bedroom.

Her heart clenched at his words and a feeling of rightness slipped through her – like a key fitting a lock – and she swallowed once before nodding.

It took only her nod of assent. Clare gasped as Blake moved at his superhuman speed, his clothes off and his body sliding behind hers in the water. She squealed as his arms came around her, pulling her back to his chest, and held her tight as he traced a kiss down the back of her neck. For a moment, he held her tightly, their breathing becoming one as Clare slowly relaxed against his body.

"I've dreamt of you," Blake said against her neck, his warm breath on her skin making her shiver. One hand traced lightly across her stomach, heat trailing in its wake. She arched against him as his hand found her breasts, slipping lightly over them in the warm water, and she squirmed in need.

"I've dreamt of you. Like this: warm, pliant, molding to my body as I gave you pleasure," Blake murmured, his hand increasing its rhythm against her sensitive breasts. Clare was shocked to find she was close to the edge. The pressure built as he continued to tease her with his words, his lips, his hands... until she gasped and went over the edge on a cry.

On her whimper of delight, Blake slipped his hand between her legs and found her, loose and languid, and stroked her gently, mercilessly, rigidly, until she gasped once more, crashing into oblivion again.

Clare wanted to bury her face in her hands in embarrassment. "Ah, well, I – um," she began, wanting to apologize for her obvious need.

"Shh," Blake said, flipping her easily in the water so that she lay across his chest, her lips near his. "I will live to give you pleasure. Every sigh you make, every moment of pleasure you take, is my own."

"Oh," Clare breathed, her eyes on his as she brought her legs up to straddle him. Feeling bold, she nipped at his bottom lip, sucking gently for a moment as his hands trailed down her waist and cupped her butt. Clare gasped into his mouth as he slid into her with one smooth movement, taking her over the edge once again, taking her far deeper than she'd gone with anyone before.

And as they rode through the darkness together, each lost in the other, the light of love shone between them and drowned out the madness of the Domnua beating at the wards.

For in this moment, the light of love outshone the dark.

CHAPTER 32

$\mathcal{C}$lare gasped as she woke, a thin thread of light seeping through the window, the early waves of pleasure rocking through her as Blake cuddled her from behind, his hands bringing her pleasure wherever they touched.

"Blake," Clare gasped as he brought her to the peak once again. Their movements were slow in the misty morning hours, as they burrowed under the sheets and explored the dips and grooves of each other's bodies, leaning into each other's warmth and delighting in new discoveries.

The night hadn't been as restful as Clare had wanted it to be. But she was surprised to find that she felt energized, like she'd swallowed a whole pot of coffee. She had no trouble springing from the bed she'd shared with Blake and heading into the bathroom for a quick shower before they hit the road.

Though the shower had turned out to take much longer once Blake had slipped in behind her.

Now, she found herself whistling in the kitchen as she put on a pot of water for tea. Blake had gone to tend to something on the property and, as the sun hadn't fully risen yet, Clare figured she was on breakfast duty.

"Ah, you look... rested," Esther said from the doorway.

Clare jumped and then immediately blushed. Turning, she busied herself with the tea. "You've a lovely home. I was able to rest, thank you," Clare said quickly.

Esther chuckled. "My sweet Matthew used to put the same blush on my face, you know," Esther said easily, and Clare almost choked.

"Um," she said.

"Sure and you don't think I can't tell when a woman's been well-loved by her man? I'm pleased you've found your way to each other. I was beginning to worry about him," Esther admitted. She pulled up a chair at the small table tucked in the corner of the kitchen, content to let Clare take care of prepping the morning tea.

"Why were you worried?"

"Well, child, he hasn't looked at another woman since he saw you. It's been a lonely ten years for him," Esther said.

The spoon Clare had been holding clattered to the floor.

"I'm sorry," Clare said immediately, bending to pick

up the spoon. "He hasn't been with another woman for ten years?"

"Well, I can't say whether he's been with anyone in that manner. But he hasn't dated anyone seriously. Nor has he talked about anyone. Anyone but you, that is. Frankly, I feel like I know you from everything he's told me about you. I'm pleased you're feeling the same way about him."

Clare turned and moved to the sink, processing the information, as she rinsed the spoon under the faucet.

"I'm not sure as I feel the way you're thinking I feel about him," Clare said cautiously, not wanting to rush too far down that path, or potentially mislead Esther into believing she was in love with Blake.

"You don't care for him, then?" Esther asked.

Clare turned and crossed her arms over her chest, leaning back against the counter as she studied Esther. Her heart wanted to shout with joy over what she felt for Blake, but her logical brain said it was too soon.

Too soon to be in love.

"I care for him. Very much. I'm just not sure that I'm, you know…" Clare said, shrugging a shoulder.

Esther's face brightened. "Ah, the silliness of youth. Wasted moments. For what? Pride? Being scared of being vulnerable? Psssh," Esther waved her hand and stood, moving to a cabinet and pulling out a glass container of muffins. "You'll know when the time is right to speak the words. It's enough for me if you promise you'll take care with his heart."

Relieved, Clare nodded and moved to take the now-steaming kettle from the stove.

"That I can promise. I'll take care with his heart. And, no matter what happens with us, I'd like for you and me to stay friends," Clare said softly.

"Friends. Isn't that something? I'd like that. I'm a gifted pen pal, you know," Esther chuckled.

Clare felt a bit of a weight ease from her heart. "Plus, you know, you're like me. Is it a sisterhood then? Like, we stick together?" she asked, pulling out a few mugs and placing them on the small table, along with the pot of tea. Settling into a chair, she looked at Esther.

"Aye, we're a sisterhood. And far more powerful than we realize. It took me a while to understand my own power. It's nice to hear that you began testing your wings as soon as you knew what you were."

"I'm surprised I have," Clare admitted, pushing her muffin around on her plate. "It's quite unlike me to believe in such matters."

"A near brush with death will often cause someone to suspend disbelief," Esther pointed out, padding in her house slippers to the table and settling down. This morning she wore a bright red sweater and soft cotton pants, with her hair braided in two neat braids on either side of her face. Take away the lines in her face and the white hair, and she could easily be thirty years younger, Clare thought as she looked into Esther's bright eyes.

"I suppose it does, doesn't it?" Clare agreed, picking the muffin apart and nibbling on a piece. "I also... I think there was a part of me that knew. I just knew I was meant for greater things. So I spent my whole life hunting down the closest thing I could figure out to what made my heart sing. Which was studying stones. And I'd convinced myself that getting a masters degree would fulfill that need in me – finding that greatness, you know? But now I see it was something entirely different that was driving me. All this time wasted." Clare sighed and picked up her cup of tea.

"Why, child, it wasn't wasted time at all. I'd say you're exactly where you're supposed to be."

Clare wasn't sure if that was true, but it was certainly nice to hear. Just as nice as it was to hear Bianca and Seamus bickering in the hallway as they made their way to the kitchen.

"Thanks for the chat. I wish we could take you with us," Clare said, smiling at Esther.

"You'll come back after you find the stone. I'll make you the best celebratory dinner you've ever had. We'll invite your parents too, and have ourselves a proper hooley. That's a promise to you – from a seer," Esther said firmly, then turned as Bianca and Seamus burst into the kitchen.

Clare sincerely hoped it was a promise she could count on.

CHAPTER 33

"You've gone and slept with him, haven't you?" Bianca asked, pulling Clare aside in the toilet. They'd stopped at a petrol station about an hour away from Esther's home. With no particular plan in mind, they'd decided to head south. It felt right to Clare, though she had no reason to give when pressed as to why she chose that direction.

Clare shot Bianca a wide-eyed look as one of the toilets flushed. Giggling, she ducked into her own stall, avoiding the question.

But to no avail, as Bianca leaned against the wall, her arms crossed over her chest, and simply waited for Clare to speak. Washing her hands, Clare glanced around before meeting Bianca's eyes in the mirror.

"I did, yes. And it was wonderful," Clare finally said.

Bianca squealed, clapping her hands together once. "I

knew it! I could tell. You were all aflutter this morning," Bianca said.

Clare blanched visibly in the mirror. "I most certainly was not all aflutter. I quite simply do not flutter about," Clare said, glaring at her friend with indignity.

"Oh, you were fluttering. But that's all right; so was I." Bianca laughed at her and Clare grinned.

"You've gone and shagged Seamus, haven't you?"

"Like I could keep my hands off of him after he hung himself out the window and shot magickal arrows at the Domnua? Please." Bianca fanned her face. "I was dying for dinner to be over last night so I could jump him."

"I'm sure he was pleased with that then," Clare laughed.

"He seemed quite happy," Bianca agreed. "But talk to me. I want details."

Clare sighed and turned to face her friend. What could she say? That she was worried she'd fallen so fast? That she wasn't sure of who she was anymore, much less whether or not she could trust her own feelings?

"It's a lot, isn't it?" Bianca asked, concern crossing her face as she studied Clare.

"It's quite a lot. I just… am struggling. How can I trust what I feel? I don't even know who I am anymore."

"You're still you. You're just an enhanced version of you. Like Clare 2.0," Bianca said, startling Clare into a laugh.

"So you're saying just embrace it, roll with it, and go with the flow?" Clare asked.

"I'm saying take that dragon for a ride and shoot lightning bolts from your hand while you're at it, Goddess," Bianca said, a wide grin splitting her face as she pulled the door open and motioned for Clare to go out in front of her. "The ride's yours for the taking."

"I'll keep that in mind," Clare demurred. She'd wondered about Blake almost incessantly since he'd kissed her at the circle of stones yesterday. It had felt like there was great meaning behind that kiss.

Clare didn't know what she wanted – from him, from the kiss, from anything really. She only knew that she didn't want to be away from him.

And maybe that was all she needed to know in this moment, Clare thought as she nodded her thanks to the man working behind the counter and stepped outside to where Blake was fueling the SUV. For a moment, she was distracted by the way the sun gleamed off of the black car, the handsome man leaning on it with his arms crossed in his leather jacket making quite a picture. One she couldn't quite believe might belong to her.

"Domnua," Bianca hissed and Clare whirled, instinctively throwing her hand out as power raced along her skin from her necklace down to her arm. Bianca, having not been distracted by Blake, had seen what Clare should have seen, a drove of fifteen or so large Domnua slipping into the parking lot behind the SUV. They moved fast, crouching low to the ground, their bodies but a silvery streak in the daylight. Clare realized they were using the sun to their advantage, slipping from ray to shimmering ray, concealing their approach.

Clare whipped her power at them and felt it snake across the parking lot. The fae shattered into a million silvery pieces before winking out of sight. Blake had barely had time to whirl and crouch, his dagger in his hand.

"Badass," Bianca commented, as they raced across the lot to the still-crouching Blake.

"You have no idea. I mean, I always knew stones had power, but, wow, just wow," Clare panted as they skidded to a stop next to Blake. Seamus brought up the rear, having seen them running across the lot.

"Is everyone okay? What did I miss?" Seamus demanded, his hands filled with bags of pretzels and snacks.

"Just Clare blasting some Domnua to smithereens," Bianca exclaimed, reaching out to help Seamus with his load.

"Far out," Seamus said, pressing a kiss to Clare's cheek. Clare just nodded as she watched Blake, who, from where she stood, looked extremely angry.

"Uh-oh," Bianca whispered as she passed Clare. "Someone's ego is out of sorts."

Clare waited while Seamus and Bianca piled into the back of the car. Finally, Blake met her eyes.

"Thanks," Blake bit out.

"Don't mention it," Clare said, her tone frosty as she turned on her heel and got into the passenger seat. Far be it from her to point out that he would have been in trouble if they hadn't come out of the station when they had. But no… Damn men and their egos.

Blake slid into the driver's seat, slamming the door louder than necessary, and gunned the car away from the station, all but leaving a trail of smoke behind them. The car remained silent and Clare crossed her arms over her chest and stuck her nose in the air. It wasn't as if she had anything to apologize for.

"Soooo," Seamus said, five minutes later when no one had broken the silence. "Did I miss something else?"

"Someone's mad that I saved him from the Domnua," Clare said, then gasped as Blake swerved to the left and pulled the car off the side of the road. Slamming his hands on the steering wheel, he glared out the window.

"I'm the Protector. I'm supposed to protect you. That's what I'm here for. You're not supposed to be the one protecting me. This is what I was worried about! I knew I should have waited to touch you – to taste you. My mind is distracted. I'm just standing there, daydreaming about your body, and I could have been killed in an instant by the Domnua. What was I thinking?" Blake burst out.

"Maybe we should leave…" Seamus began, but Bianca cut him off and shook her head.

"No way am I missing this," she said in a stage-whisper.

And had Blake not been so intensely angry, Clare might have found humor in the situation. Instead, his words were like bullets, each one hitting her and burning to her core.

"It wasn't me who kissed you at the stone circle yesterday! It wasn't me who slipped into the bathroom while I was in the tub!" Clare shot back.

"Oh, this is getting good," Seamus whispered from the back seat and Bianca elbowed him in the ribs.

"I was helpless not to touch you," Blake seethed.

"Don't play the victim here, buddy, because I simply won't allow it. You wanted what you wanted and you got it," Clare seethed right back, feeling anger seep into the warmth she had felt for Blake earlier today.

"Aye, I wanted you – against my own better sense. I knew it would be suicide to touch you," Blake said, slamming his hand on the steering wheel again.

Clare looked out the window and blinked back the tears that threatened to overtake her. She'd been stupid to open herself to him – especially when they were in such a vulnerable position. It would be best if she played it cool and moved forward – for the sake of the team.

"Hey now, don't you think you're being a little harsh?" Bianca interjected, coming to Clare's defense.

"It's fine, Bianca," Clare glanced over her shoulder with a smile for her friend, before turning a cool gaze on Blake. "We had some fun. Tensions were high and I needed an itch scratched. So, thanks for providing the scratch. Your services will no longer be needed."

Seamus whistled long and low from the back seat, so Clare knew that she had played her hand well. Though her heart twisted with the words, it was the only way to protect them all and stay on track with the quest. She'd deal with the fallout after she found the stone.

"Is that the way of it then, Doc?" Blake asked, bitterness lacing his voice.

"Aye, that's most certainly the way of it," Clare said, turning to look out the window and trying her damnedest to not crawl across the car and jump in his lap. She wanted to tell him no – of course it wasn't true. But he was hurting her and this was the only way she knew to stay strong. Keep a professional distance – she'd learned it for her career, and now she would apply it to this job, too.

After all, this was the biggest job of her life.

Framing it like that helped to dull the edges of the pain, Clare thought, as Blake silently pulled the car back onto the road. She'd never have fraternized with a colleague at work – so what had made her think it would be okay to do so on this mission?

"Ah, I hate to interrupt, but does anyone know where we're going?" Seamus asked after a few more minutes of driving in silence. Clare ignored Blake's sigh of frustration as she looked back at Seamus and shrugged.

"I actually had a thought about that, while you two were yelling and pretending like you don't care about each other," Bianca said cheerfully.

Clare's mouth fell open and, turning, she glared at her friend.

"It's not that we don't care. It's just that we're going to keep a professional distance from now on. There's work to be done," Clare said, enunciating carefully and shooting daggers at Bianca with her eyes.

"Sure, whatever you say, boss. But here's my thought – I was kicking the latest clue around in my head, and I think I figured out where we have to go."

"Where's that?" Blake finally spoke.

"Mt. Brandon," Bianca said, beaming.

Clare just shook her head in confusion as Blake cursed long and low.

"Of course," Blake said.

"I'm missing something?" Clare asked, looking between the two.

"What my beauty here has figured out," Seamus said, "is that the clue talked about the saint walking his path in darkness. Another name for Mt. Brandon is the Saint's Path. It used to be a Christian pilgrimage site. Has stations of the cross all the way to the top of the mountain. Makes perfect sense. The clue was being quite literal," he finished, wrapping his arm around Bianca and giving her a little squeeze. Her face flushed in pleasure at his praise and Clare found herself being a little jealous. Why couldn't she and Blake be easygoing like that?

Because there was no 'she and Blake,' she reminded herself, turning around and crossing her arms over her chest.

"To the Saint's Path we go then."

CHAPTER 34

The air in the car stayed tense for the next hour while Clare and Bianca worked on their iPads, bouncing theories off each other.

"What do we know about the Saint's Path?" Seamus asked, the bag of pretzels rattling as he dug into them. Blake's jaw twitched at the sound, and it gave Clare great pleasure to reach for a handful of pretzels and eat them clumsily in his immaculate car.

Hey, nobody said she didn't have a mean streak.

To his credit, Blake stayed quiet and focused on driving. Clare suspected he was still upset about missing the Domnua earlier; she watched as his eyes scanned his surroundings constantly.

Everywhere but her, that is.

So what? Clare thought, miffed that he'd accepted her reframing of the beautiful night they'd had together. It served her right, she supposed. She shouldn't have dismissed their time together so casually. But hadn't he been the one to get mad that she'd distracted him?

The endless loop of annoyance in her mind made Clare want to scream. Instead, she sighed heavily as she took notes.

"They say that Saint Brendan once lived there. It was a popular pilgrimage site for the early Christians. There are crosses all the way to the top. It's a nice walk, that's for sure," Bianca said.

"But nothing about the fae? No magickal history?" Clare asked.

"None that I'm finding on the internet – with the limited time we want to be on the internet and all. But that doesn't mean there isn't. It's more likely to be in some of my old manuscripts than anywhere else," Bianca said.

Clare's phone beeped with an incoming text. She knew Blake preferred her to keep the phone turned off, but since she was feeling defiant today, she'd turned it back on.

"I just heard from Fiona. She's instructed us to go to Grace's Cove and get a meal and a pint at a Gallagher's Pub. They'll put us up for the night and we can start our climb tomorrow."

"It's a lunar eclipse tomorrow," Seamus said.

Clare slanted a look at him. "How do you know that?"

"I follow astrology," Seamus said with a smile.

"Really?" Bianca asked. "Are our signs compatible?"

"I don't need a horoscope sign to be telling me if we're compatible or not," Seamus said and Bianca giggled.

Clare rolled her eyes and wished to be out of this car as soon as possible.

"We'll climb it at the eclipse then," Blake said, his voice tense.

They all paused; they were the first words Blake had spoken in over an hour.

"At night?" Bianca squeaked.

"The saint walks his path in darkness," Blake quoted and they all fell silent. His words struck a chord of truth.

"He's right. And what's darker than a lunar eclipse?" Clare asked.

"Well, technically, the day after a new moon would be the darkest," Seamus began, but then held up his hand. "But yes, it seems poetic and right. I think tomorrow night we hike."

"Great, just lovely. I don't even have hiking boots," Bianca complained.

Seamus hugged her again. "I'll help you. We're a team, remember?"

Clare stared out the window as the road climbed and wound through the hills toward the coast, her mind on the word 'team.' She wondered what it would take to get them all back on even ground again.

Maybe a pint and some pub food would do the trick.

She certainly hoped so. Because if they went up the side of the mountain like this, there was a good chance they wouldn't be coming down.

CHAPTER 35

*B*lake fumed the entire way into Grace's Cove. He was feeling annoyed, angry at Clare, and most importantly, mad at himself.

Yeah, he'd really screwed up.

Blake couldn't decide which he was madder about – blaming Clare for distracting him from his job, or the fact that she had been forced to protect him from the Domnua. The very thought of it made his stomach churn in anger.

It was his job – his oath – his sole purpose was to defend against Domnua. For Clare to protect him, while he'd idly daydreamed, was about as sacrilegious as it could get. If his grandfather had been alive and caught wind of it, he'd never have lived it down.

It brought shame to his name, his role, and all the Protectors that had come before him.

Yet, he'd been helpless not to fall for Clare. She embodied everything he'd ever wanted in a woman – a sharp mind, a bruising sense of humor, and a body that curved in all the right places. He'd been mooning over her for years, and it had all just come to a head.

Having her in his family home, and taking her to the circle – well, it had pushed him over the edge. It had been stupid to take her up to the stones, Blake thought, as he crested another hill and finally caught sight of the coast.

A kiss at the circle was a pledge – of eternal love, of protection, of a promise to be hers forever. Blake wondered if she'd felt the magick curl around them when he'd kissed her.

If she knew just how much her words had hurt him when she'd lashed out at him in the car.

Though, in all fairness, he hadn't told her that he'd pledged himself to her. For all Clare knew, he was simply fulfilling his job duties. And perhaps it was better for them all that he hadn't. If she truly thought he was just another fling, well, he'd go lick his wounds in private, then.

And mourn her for the rest of his life.

CHAPTER 36

They rolled into Grace's Cove in mid-afternoon, the winter sun shining its pale light over a cheerful village tucked in the curve of a line of stunning coastal cliffs. Houses and shops clambered over each other for space, presenting a charming mix of colors and shapes. All roads wound down to the harbor, where many boats were bundled up for the winter. Clare presumed the town made its money from fishing and tourism, both of which would offer slim pickings in the winter season.

"It's a darling town," Bianca said from the backseat.

"Aye, I imagine it's quite lovely in the summer with the tourists on holiday and the boats out in the harbor," Clare agreed.

"Will Fiona be at the pub?"

"No, they're still in Dublin. We're on our own, it seems," Clare said, turning to scan the streets. "I think it's up this way, at least based on my map."

Sure enough, they wound along a one-way street and stopped in front of a large building with a cheerful sign proclaiming it to be Gallagher's Pub.

"This looks nice," Bianca said as Blake parked the car in a small alley to the side of the building.

"Aye, it does. It will be nice to have a hot meal and a pint," Seamus agreed.

Clare said nothing as they exited the car, but she waited while Blake did some sort of magick. She felt the shimmer of it slide over her as he warded the car.

She opened her mouth to say something, but Blake strode right past her – not even glancing at her.

So much for trying to make amends, Clare thought, miffed at his attitude. And if he was supposed to be protecting her, shouldn't he be waiting for her? Annoyed at everything, Clare hurried to catch up as they reached the front door of the pub.

THE PUB WAS empty but for a pint-sized woman sitting at a long wooden bar that lined one side of the bar. Tables, booths, and a tiny stage to the right showed that they packed a regular crowd. Pretty landscape pictures and beer and whiskey signs covered the walls; the pub had a nice, warm ambiance that felt immediately inviting.

"Good afternoon," the woman said, smiling at them from under a crop of dark curls, her pretty green eyes smiling at them in invitation.

"Cait?" Clare asked, raising an eyebrow at her in question.

"That's me and this is my fine establishment," Cait said, sweeping her arm out to indicate the empty pub. "Don't be fooled by the empty space. We'll be packed in about an hour."

"I'm sure you will be. Fiona sent us," Clare said, following Cait as she walked to the bar. Cait ducked under the pass-through to stand behind it.

"Ah, yes, she did text me – which is something I'm still not used to," Cait laughed, and automatically began building a Guinness.

"Texting?" Bianca asked, sliding onto a stool.

"Fiona texting. I'm not used to her using technology like that." Cait shrugged, then raised an eyebrow at Clare as she pointed at her. "Drink?"

"A cider is fine," Clare said, and Bianca nodded for the same.

"I'm assuming Guinness for the men?" Cait asked.

Both men nodded as they all took seats at the bar. Blake sat at the far end from Clare and it took everything in her power not to roll her eyes.

"You'll be needing a place to stay then?" Cait asked.

"Aye, if that's not too much trouble."

"My husband owns a lot of real estate in town. We've got a little bed and breakfast that we keep open for passersby, friends, people who've had too much to drink and the like. I'll show it to you later on; you're welcome to stay as long as needed. Any friend of Fiona's and all...

Though she didn't say how you knew her?" Cait asked, her eyes zeroing in on Clare.

Clare got a distinctly odd feeling, as though Cait was trying to pry at her mind.

Cait's eyes widened ever so slightly, and Clare realized that she was, in fact, reading her mind. Clare could feel the gentle tug of her intrusion.

"Find what you were looking for?" Clare asked coldly, but instead of looking embarrassed, Cait threw her head back and laughed, her short mop of curls bouncing around her face.

"What's happening?" Seamus asked, looking between Clare and Cait.

Cait slid Clare her cider. "That one's on the house. Cousin."

"*Sláinte,*" Clare said, tipping her drink at Cait before sipping it. So this was another branch of the family Fiona had told her about – though she'd conveniently left out the fact that they seemed to have their own sort of powers.

"I missed something," Bianca decided and Cait beamed at her.

"Since I'm assuming you're all on the quest that my family and I recently learned about, I'll be going ahead and telling you that I can read minds."

Bianca's mouth fell open, but as always with her, the shock didn't last long before the questions tumbled out.

"Isn't that awful when you have a full pub?"

"Aye. I've learned to shield it," Cait said as she topped off the pints of Guinness and slid them to the men.

"So you can just turn it off and on?" Bianca asked.

"Something like that," Cait agreed and then waved her hand as the door opened and a group of men piled in.

"Let me serve them and then we'll be getting a hot meal and a good rest in for you before your climb tomorrow," Cait said easily. She threw a look over her shoulder at Bianca. "And I probably have some hiking boots that will fit you."

"All right!" Bianca fist-pumped the air and Clare chuckled. Perhaps having cousins with extrasensory abilities would come in handy. It felt weird, this concept of having an extended family she didn't know about. From being an only child with no cousins to finding out she was a part of something so much more – well, it was proving to be a very enlightening week.

Cait hadn't lied. Within the hour, the pub was packed with locals all wanting a hot meal and a pint after a day's work. Judging from the conversations she overheard, work included everything from farming to the local market. Clare nursed her single cider and a glass of water while she ate a decidedly delicious beef stew and allowed the conversation to flow around her.

Bianca nudged her.

"Blake said to tell you we shouldn't stay too late tonight. It's harder to watch for, you know, in a pub environment. Plus, if they do follow us in here, we don't want to bust up Cait's pretty pub."

Clare nodded, though she was a little annoyed that Blake had used a game of telephone to pass the message down to her. She was about to signal Cait when someone blocked her view.

A young man, probably a few years younger than her, with broad shoulders – from working the farm, presumably – sandy blonde hair, and laughing blue eyes smiled at her cheerfully.

"Sure and that's a pretty face I haven't seen yet in this pub. The name's Garrett," he said, holding his hand out. Clare took it automatically, and was startled when Garrett brought her hand to his lips for a kiss.

"Clare," she said, snatching her hand back and trying not to blush.

"You're not from around here then?" Garrett asked, settling in for a chat, his eyes sizing her up appreciatively.

"Blake's getting angry," Bianca hissed in her ear.

That decided Clare. Turning her back completely, she smiled brightly at Garrett.

"From Dublin, actually. Clifden originally though."

"Ah, a west coaster like myself then. Grow up in Clifden, or outside?"

"On a farm," Clare said, smiling at him.

"A girl after me own heart," Garrett said, tapping his palm on his chest. "Say, can I buy you a drink then?"

Clare debated saying yes for a moment, but decided to decline. She was about to say so when a voice spoke for her.

"The lady is finished drinking for the evening," Blake said over her shoulder, his tone menacing.

Even though she knew she'd been trying to goad him,

Clare was astounded that he would be this rude. Turning, she frowned at him, but his eyes held Garrett's.

"Sure thing, though I think the lady can decide for herself. Am I right, lad?" Garrett said, baring his teeth in a hint of a smile.

"I'm done. And not because he said so, but because I am done and we were about to leave. Nice to have met you, Garrett, but my friends and I must be going."

"Perhaps another time, then," Garrett said, picking up her hand and pressing a kiss – to her palm this time, deliberately provoking Blake, who all but growled over her shoulder. As he slipped away into the crowd, Clare turned to glare at Blake.

"He was being perfectly nice. I'm capable of turning down advances. I worked in a pub, remember?" Clare asked hotly, then brought her voice down when she noticed people glancing her way.

Blake just looked past her shoulder and nodded, signaling Cait.

"Ready to go?" Cait asked cheerfully.

"Aye, we're ready." Blake spoke for them, though Clare stubbornly wanted to stay for another pint now.

Cait's eyes met Clare's briefly. Amusement danced in them before she waved for them to follow her. Blake stayed one step behind Clare, nudging her through the crowd, as they made their way to the back door.

Sure, *now* he wanted to walk with her, Clare thought, annoyance washing through her.

They followed Cait from the pub, across a little courtyard, and over to a building next door. Cait unlocked the front door and led them up the stairs to a small hallway with two doors.

"Two bedrooms only. But two double beds in each so girls and guys can sleep separately," Cait said easily, unlocking both doors and then sliding a glance at the group. "Or, you know, however it is you want to divide it up."

"Cait, thank you for this. We really appreciate it," Clare said.

"A word?" Cait asked her.

Clare nodded, glancing back at Blake, whose eyes burned into hers, before following Cait down the stairs.

Stepping onto the front stoop, Cait closed the door behind them for privacy. "That man has it bad for you," she said without preamble.

"Blake?" Clare asked, and then rolled her eyes. "He says I'm a distraction."

"Of course you are. He's mad for you," Cait said, a smile on her face.

"More like mad at me. He can't get over the fact that I..." Clare debated how to frame what she wanted to say about the Domnua and then watched Cait's eyes go wide.

"Do I need to protect my family?" Cait whispered, having read everything she needed to know from Clare's mind.

"They're not after you. Only me. And other Seekers." Clare shrugged. "It would do them more harm than good to go after regular civilians. It would cause a panic.

Make their lives more difficult. Though, if you've got the sight, it's the silver-eyed ones you're to be watching out for."

Cait nodded her thanks, her eyes serious.

"You hike tomorrow night?"

"Aye."

"Make things right with your man. You're going to need his strength. Come to the pub for breakfast tomorrow. I'll see if I can gather anything else to help you on your way."

"You've a kind heart, Cait. Thank you," Clare said, impulsively reaching out and gathering Cait into a hug. She wasn't much of a hugger, and judging by the way Cait tentatively hugged her back, Cait wasn't either. But it felt right and it was nice to know an extended branch of her family.

"When this is over, you'll come back here and take a holiday. Grace's Cove has some magickal spots," Cait said, smiling up at her before slipping away to go back to the pub. Clare glanced around the now dark village with windows shining like bright beacons all the way up into the hills. Seeing nothing out of sorts, she climbed the stairs.

Blake leaned on the wall next to an open doorway.

"You're in here."

"Fine," Clare said, breezing past him. She expected to see Bianca in the room. When she saw Blake's bag instead, she whirled around – to find Blake slamming and locking the door.

"I'm not sleeping in here with you," Clare said, her hands on her hips.

"Fine, sleep in the hallway then. I'm getting some rest," Blake bit out.

Clare's mouth dropped open. Where was the kind man who had bared his heart to her the night before? Furious, she dug in her bag for a t-shirt and her makeup kit and headed to the bathroom tucked off the room.

When she returned, Blake was already under the covers of his bed, his back turned to hers.

Fine, Clare thought, slamming her bag down and making as much noise as she felt like. Climbing into bed, she flipped the light off, and turned her back on Blake.

Staring at the wall, she promised herself she wouldn't cry.

And bit down on her lip when the first tear dropped anyway.

CHAPTER 37

*B*lake stared at the moonlight spilling in from the single window on his side of the room. It was taking every ounce of his willpower not to slip into bed next to Clare and show her that everything she'd said about him just scratching an itch was a lie. They both knew there was more to it than that.

So why was he sitting here sulking then?

When he heard a muffled sniff from her bed, Blake sat straight up. Was she crying? He could deal with pretty much anything in this world – except tears from someone he loved. It went back to the days of Esther crying when she remembered his parents. Blake never wanted to see those he loved hurting.

Blake curled his hands into fists as he stared at the wall and counted to ten. Maybe he was wrong.

Another muffled sniff had him grinding his teeth.

But he went to her – because he was helpless to resist

her cries, helpless to withstand being separated from her, helpless to not be touching her when they were in the same room together.

Clare stiffened when he lifted the covers and slid into the bed next to her, wrapping his arm around her and pulling her back to his chest. Neither said a word and Blake simply held her until her body relaxed and her cries softened. Stroking her arm, he soothed her with nonsense words until she finally lay pliant against him, curled into his body, their warmth and closeness soothing Blake's soul, too.

"I wasn't going to let him buy me a drink," Clare said finally.

Blake laughed into her hair, inhaling her scent. "I wouldn't have let him buy you a drink," Blake said.

"I can make my own decisions," Clare bristled, but Blake just pulled her more tightly against his chest.

"You're mine, my love. It's best you remember that," Blake said, then laughed again when Clare tried to squirm from his arms.

"You aren't the boss of me," Clare said hotly.

"No, I'm not. But I am in love with you," Blake said, and Clare went limp in his arms.

They lay like that for a moment, both absorbing the truth of his words.

"It hurt me... the way you acted. After the night we shared," Clare said stiffly.

"I know. I was embarrassed that you had to save me.

My pride was wounded," Blake said, nuzzling into her neck.

"I can see that. I'm sorry I reacted the way I did," Clare said, her words like balm to his wounded heart. "I was just trying to protect myself because I saw you pulling away from me. And I lashed back at you."

"Thank you," Blake said, and though he desperately wanted to hear the words of love said back to him, he sensed that she wasn't yet ready to say them.

What was love if you couldn't be understanding? Deciding not to push, telling himself it didn't matter if she said 'I love you' back, he turned her so he could find her lips with his own.

And poured his anguish and his heart into their love-making. Because even if she couldn't say it with words, Blake could feel her love pulse from her with every touch. Every whisper. Every kiss.

It had to be enough.

For now.

CHAPTER 38

*C*lare awoke to a naked man handing her a cup of steaming tea. She gulped as her eyes traveled up his muscular body all the way to his cheerful face.

"Thank you," Clare said, clearing her throat and sitting up against the headboard, pulling the sheet with her to keep her naked body covered. She blushed as she recalled her tears of the night before, the vulnerability, and the incredibly intimate lovemaking that had followed.

She felt exposed in the light of day and buried her face in the steaming cup of tea.

Blake studied her for a moment, while she sipped her tea and stared at the bed.

"Feeling shy today?"

Clare glanced up, surprised at how astute he was.

"A bit," she admitted.

"I've just the cure for that," Blake said, taking the cup of tea from her gently and placing it on the bedside stand before yanking the sheet off of her too quickly for her to grab it.

"Blake!" Clare squealed, covering her ladybits with her hands.

"Never hide yourself from me," Blake said and pounced.

Later, Clare had trouble wiping the smile from her face as she used the postage-stamp-sized shower and went through her morning routine. Even though she knew they had to conquer a mountain – quite literally – this evening, she felt like she'd personally already conquered a pretty big one.

Her eyes met her reflection in the mirror as she swept on the barest hint of makeup. If she was being honest with herself, she hadn't totally conquered the mountain.

Because she was still holding back those three little words and their very huge impact. Glaring at herself in the mirror, she ran a comb through her damp hair and wondered why it was so hard to admit to him her feelings. Was it too soon? Was there a perfect time frame of when it was okay to tell someone you loved them? Or what if it wasn't love? What if it was just the high-stress situation and they were reacting in the most natural way to the stress of it all?

Questions churned through her brain, but one thing she was certain about was that she did feel a bit guilty about not telling him how she felt. Idly, she wondered if telling him that she cared for him would cut it.

She laughed as she imagined just how well that would fly.

She'd already learned her lesson about male egos yesterday. It was best not to poke the beast, Clare thought as she left the bathroom and smiled at Blake, who was sitting on the bed.

"I would've joined you in the shower, but..." Blake said.

"I know. It's tiny," Clare said with another smile. She tucked her dirty clothes and toiletry bag in her duffel.

"Bianca and Seamus already walked over to the pub. We're all set to go. If you're ready, that is," Blake said, smiling gently at her. Today he wore fitted black jeans, a plaid shirt under a wool sweater, and his leather jacket. He was so handsome it was almost painful for Clare; a part of her wanted to stay there and undress him all over again.

"Aye, I'm ready. Though, if I were to admit it, which I'm not, I would say that I'm nervous about later," Clare said, rubbing the aquamarine ring on her finger.

"That's a good thing. Nerves give you an edge. I'd be worried if you weren't nervous," Blake said, rising and putting his arm around her shoulder. As they left the room, Clare marveled at how easy he was with her – with touching her and just being comfortable with her. Even though she hadn't said she loved him.

Clare wondered if he was giving her the gift of time. Or the space that he had once requested of her.

Either way, she was grateful that the awkwardness of yesterday had eased, and in the wan light of the grey

January morning, they made their way to the pub at ease with each other.

"Cait got us supplies!" Bianca exclaimed as soon as they entered the pub. The three of them stood by a table where a few packs were laid out.

"Good morning to you too," Clare said, flashing them a smile.

Cait ran her gaze over the two of them, then nodded, sending a quick wink of understanding to Clare.

"Just some basics for climbing a mountain at night in January. Some grips for your boots, as there is shale up top and that can get slippery. Headlamps, some backup flashlights, emergency warming blankets, first aid kits, and some food rations and water."

"That's... incredible," Clare decided, looking down at everything.

"I certainly wouldn't be doing my part if I let you go up there unassisted, now would I?" Cait shook her head.

"I'm happy to reimburse you," Blake began, but Cait waved at him.

"You're family. Now, I've got Patrick cooking up a full Irish in the kitchen. You'll be wanting to get a head start today, so you'll get at least halfway up in the light," Cait said as Clare looked at her team.

Her team. Warmth filled her heart as she looked at them all – so willing to put their lives on the line to find this mythological stone.

"Do you think that's a good idea? Get a head start during the day?"

"Makes sense to me," Bianca said cheerfully as she picked up a headlamp and adjusted it to her head. Clare felt dread fill her as she looked at her easygoing friend, who had no magickal powers at all, and suddenly felt horrible about bringing her on this mission.

"Bianca, I think it's best if you stay here," Clare said, putting her hand on her friend's shoulder. "I feel like I'm putting you at an unfair disadvantage."

Bianca's mouth gaped open. "Sure and you can't think you'll be leaving me behind?" she gasped.

"It's just that… I've got a bad feeling about this. And you don't have any powers. Why would I lead you into danger like this?"

"You're not leading me. I'm going of my own accord. You're welcome to try and stop me, but I'll be on that mountain tonight whether you take me or not," Bianca said, a mutinous expression on her face. "I'll make Cait drive me."

Clare glanced at Cait who just nodded in agreement.

"You're sure? You're really, really sure?"

"I'm sure. I'm fighting for my life too – not just for you to find the stone. Remember that," Bianca said stiffly, her pride mortally offended.

Clare sighed and threw her arms around Bianca.

"I love you, okay? You're like my sister. I'm just worried."

Bianca sighed into her neck and hugged her back.

"Don't pull that shite with me. You know I'm all in."

CHAPTER 39

*C*lare thought about that concept – going all in –
as they began their hike later that afternoon.
Mount Brandon, about a forty-minute drive from Grace's
Cove, had several access points. Deciding to follow the
traditional pilgrimage path, they'd arrived at a gravel car
park with a little stream and a sign at the base of the path.
Had there been no sign, it would have looked like every
other green pasture with a stone fence in Ireland. It was
only when Clare shaded her eyes and looked up that she
saw the first of the crosses marking the pathway up the
side of the foothills.

They'd chosen to hike single file, with Blake leading
the front, the girls in the middle, and Seamus bringing up
the rear. At the moment, they walked in silence, appreciating the scenery and staying alert for any traps.

Hopping a sheep fence, they kept climbing up the
rolling green hill. A look over her shoulder showed the

promise of a spectacular view if they reached the top, as the green foothills rolled away into nothing but stunning ocean vistas.

Turning back, Clare stayed focused on where she was stepping and went back to her thoughts about Bianca and her fearlessness. She'd always been that way – or at least as long as Clare had known her. Bianca exhibited an exuberance for life, and whether it was her latest class or her latest boyfriend, she always jumped in with both feet. Clare, by contrast, always dipped her toe in carefully, testing the temperature of the water first. She wondered what it was about herself that didn't allow her to be so free with her emotions.

What was she really scared of?

She'd never been in love before, and aside from Bianca and her parents, had nobody that she loved unconditionally. Maybe Branna, perhaps, but she was still her boss so there were some conditions there.

Was that why she couldn't say the words to Blake? Words that she knew he wanted to hear?

Feeling slightly ashamed that she hadn't allowed herself to speak the words to Blake earlier today, she made a promise to herself that when this was all over, she'd be as honest about her feelings with Blake – and with everyone – as she could. No more getting caught up in her clinical science mind. Instead, it was time to embrace this new Clare, and allow her emotions to have more say in her life.

"Do you feel it?" Blake whispered over his shoulder

and Clare glanced up, surprised that he could read her mind.

"I can," Seamus said from the back and Clare rolled her eyes at herself. They weren't talking about her thoughts – there was a palpable press of magick in the air. It seemed to grow thicker as they trudged along, passing the stations of the cross, each one numbered. When they reached number eight, they paused.

"Let's shelter," Blake called over the increasingly high wind.

Clare nodded, keeping her head down as the gusts threatened to pull her cap right off her head. At this elevation on the mountain, the land was steeper, but there were also large rocky outcroppings that jutted straight up from the side of the mountain. Blake led them around one taller than their heads, and they were immediately sheltered from the wind.

"Let's settle in here for a moment," Blake said, dropping his pack. Another large outcropping ran parallel to them, forming a makeshift shelter and protecting their spot from any prying eyes.

Though from the press of magick she felt on her skin, Clare doubted there was anywhere they would really be able to hide on this mountain.

"They're here, aren't they?" Clare asked quietly and Bianca whipped her head around, her eyes wide in her face, a dagger in her hand.

"I haven't seen any Domnua yet, but the Danula are here," Blake said.

"The Danula!" Bianca gasped.

"Our brethren," Seamus said with a flash of a smile on his wind-reddened face.

"We've got backup," Blake agreed, and Clare was surprised to feel the press of tears at her eyes. They weren't in this alone.

"Oh... oh, I'm so glad. I've been so worried. Just us against god knows what," Clare said, pressing her hands to her eyes and willing the tears away. Bianca bumped her shoulder with her own.

"Hey, we've never been in this alone. I think they were just biding their time, deciding when to show themselves, you know? Like saving the big guns for the final battle type deal?"

"Is that what you think this is? The final battle?" Clare asked.

"Feels right. Well, at least the final battle for our leg of it," Blake said.

"The clues seem spot-on. The lunar eclipse feels right; I think all signs point to go," Seamus agreed.

"But what are we looking for? I don't even know what the stone looks like. I mean, do I need to run all over the mountain and pick up stones until one sings?" Clare asked, exasperation lacing her voice. Feeling unprepared and out of her element were two of her least favorite feelings.

"If it was that easy, the stone would have been found centuries ago," Bianca pointed out.

Clare sighed, wrapping her arms around her knees as she watched the sun dip below the edge of the ocean.

"And what if I can't find it?"

There. She'd said her greatest fear. Aside from herself and all of her friends dying on this mountain tonight.

"You will," Bianca said confidently.

Clare turned to meet her friend's eyes. "How can you be so sure?"

"I've never known you to not get what you go after," Bianca said easily, turning back to look at the water. Gasping, she pointed. "Look!"

The full moon rose as the sun sank, two glorious spheres bypassing each other in the sky, always friends, but destined never to meet.

They watched in silence as the last rays of the sun's light shot across the wintry grey sea, golden spears of light in the encroaching darkness.

"Look. In the light," Seamus breathed.

And when Clare squinted, she made out what looked like arches and swirls, pinging back and forth from beam to beam, racing across the water to the base of the mountain.

"The Danula have arrived," Blake said, his voice positively cheerful.

"And so have the Domnua," Clare whispered, pointing to the silvery grey fog lurking in the dips of the foothills, creeping over the rounded green crests, advancing slowly up the side of the mountain.

"We must go. Now. I feel it," Blake said, standing. "The battle begins at our feet."

And so it was, Clare thought, her heart pounding in her

chest, as she saw the golden and purple beams of light slip into the silvery fog and what looked like bolts of lightning zipping through the gray. It reminded Clare of what it was like to fly above a storm in an airplane, looking down at tumultuous gray clouds with brilliant bolts of gold and white light.

Except the fog was the evil fae and the golden bolts of light were the good.

Turning her back, Clare began to climb, the loose shale of the path slowing their steps, the increasing ascent of the fae making Clare want to race forward.

"Take your time," Blake said, snatching her arm as she slipped on a particularly precarious piece of shale. She gasped as it clattered over a ledge and fell, shattering in pieces down the side of the mountain.

"You'll do us no good if you die," Blake said, his hand still on her arm as he guided her.

"I'm so nervous. I feel like I have to race to the top but I don't know what to do or where to go."

"The truth always reveals itself," Bianca called back, reminding her of the clue, her voice but a tinny sound on the wind. They bent forward, their hiking poles digging into the side of the mountain as they made their way up, a meter at a time, while the battle raged fiercely below them.

"There's a shelter. Believed to be St. Brendan's home. If we find it in time, we can protect ourselves while we wait for the eclipse and plan our next step," Bianca called, the words being torn from her mouth by the wind. Clare nodded, and they pushed forward, their headlamps shining small circles of light ahead of them.

The cold – oh, such cold – was beginning to seep into her bones. Clare kept her head down and wished dully for the wind to stop, just for a moment. What were they doing climbing a mountain in the middle of winter? If the wind didn't fling them off the side of the mountain, the Domnua would certainly be happy to lend a hand.

What felt like several hours later – though was probably only one hour – Clare was close to giving up. She just needed to stop, to lay down, to cover her face from the punishing wind – then she heard a shout from Seamus.

"Here! It's here," Seamus called and Clare looked up to see his flashlight illuminating the stone walls of a house with no roof. It wasn't full shelter, but the stones had been there for a long time and certainly weren't in danger of blowing over tonight. They'd be sheltered on three sides and be able to look out over the mountain. It was the best they could hope for. Clare stepped eagerly behind a wall and gasped with happiness at the relief from the near-constant gusts of wind.

"I can't believe we've made it this far," Bianca puffed, her cheeks red and her eyes bright with excitement. "I didn't think I'd make it. But I held my own!"

"Aye, that you did," Clare agreed, taking a swig of water from the bottle that had been tucked in the side of her pack. Easing down to the ground, she leaned against a wall and studied the scene before them.

"The battle's closer," Blake observed.

It was true, too. As they'd slowly made their way higher on the mountain, the battle between the light and dark had raged on, and was now inching closer to where they were positioned on the mountain.

A soft wash of light from the moon illuminated the creep of the battle, and Clare shivered as she realized just how close it had advanced.

"They'll have sentries who run ahead—" Blake began, then Bianca pointed.

"The eclipse! It's starting!"

Clare's mouth went dry as the light of the moon began to be slowly swallowed by the darkness.

CHAPTER 40

"Arm yourselves," Blake said immediately. They all stood, strapping various bits of weaponry to their bodies. Seamus had his magickal bow and arrow at the ready and Bianca held both a machete and a dagger in her hands.

Clare held only her small dagger. Perhaps its size was understated, but the power she felt pulsing from it told her not to underestimate its strength.

"I must go," Clare said, suddenly certain of it. She couldn't stay there with her friends; the Domnua were after her. And something was pulling her, tugging her out of the shelter and further toward the tip of the mountain. The stones at her neck and on her ring began to pulse gently as the moon slowly slipped into shadow.

"You must stay here where I can protect you," Blake shouted over the increasingly loud howls of the Domnua, carried to them on the gusts of the wind.

"No." Clare shook her head. "I have to go."

Stepping from the shelter, Clare was almost bowled over by the wind. Turning, she began to press further up the path and gasped when a hand grabbed the hem of her coat.

"Bianca!" Clare said, turning to look at her friend.

"You don't go alone," Bianca gasped.

Clare looked past her to see Seamus and Blake bringing up the rear. Unable to argue, tears pricking her eyes, Clare pressed on, following only her intuition as she scanned desperately for some sign of the stone.

Clare gasped.

The wind had stopped. For one heart-stopping moment, Clare turned to smile at her friends in her relief at no longer having to battle the wind.

Only to see thousands of Domnua and Danula steps behind them.

They were no longer in front of the storm.

They were in the storm.

Blake was already turning, his sword out, as the battle tumbled over them, encompassing them instantly. Clare gasped and jumped back as a silver Domnua, spiky wings jutting from his back, flitted at her with a spear – only to be shattered by a golden warrior Danula, a brilliant violet shield on his arm, who stepped in front of her.

"Go," the warrior ordered.

Clare kept going – climbing to what, she did not know.

And as the last shreds of light from the moon were shrouded, Clare began to fight, jabbing and pirouetting as

Domnua shot at her, relentlessly pursuing her as she raced further up the side of the mountain. It became almost mechanical, her dagger ripping into flesh that disintegrated into a silvery streak, taking a few more steps before another would jump her. The Danula were fighting a noble battle, but Clare began to grow weary, convinced they would never overcome the constant deluge of Domnua.

Clare screeched and doubled over as she felt a shock of pain in her side. Turning, she slammed her dagger into a Domnua who had gotten too close, his knife slicing into her soft skin. A freezing pain began to creep into her side. Clare wondered dully if his knife was poisoned before she turned to find Bianca being backed up, a step at a time, by a huge Domnua, his deadly sword held aloft.

Blake, standing on a ledge and trying desperately to reach her, was being swarmed by five Domnua.

"No!" Clare screamed, raising her hand to throw a blast of power at Blake as she dove with all of her might in front of Bianca. The sword hung suspended in the air for a second, before it came down and pierced the aquamarine stone of her necklace, shattering it and driving its blade into her chest.

The last things she saw as she fell from the cliff were Bianca's and Blake's horrified expressions, frozen forever in her memory, as she slid into darkness.

CHAPTER 41

a brilliant light pressed against her eyelids. Clare moaned and turned away from it, not wanting to come out of the dark. She'd felt no pain when she was there. But now the pain ran up her chest and through her heart, making her gasp for breath.

Cracking her eyelids open, she gasped.

"I'm dead," Clare said as she stared at the heavenly form before her.

A goddess, most certainly, as there was nothing else this beautiful angel could be. With flowing locks of pure white, and brilliant blue eyes, and an otherworldly beauty that made Clare want to weep with joy, she was clearly in the presence of a much, much higher power.

"You're in between." The voice, like a million harps playing at once, whispered over her skin, soothing her.

"Bianca? Blake? Did they make it?" Clare gasped,

holding her hand to the freely-bleeding wound on her chest.

"Let's see for ourselves, shall we?" the Goddess asked, smiling at her and waving a hand. The white clouds dissipated and Clare could look down at the battle, still raging on the side of the mountain.

Seamus, Bianca, and Blake were still alive and holding their own, though the looks on their faces tore fresh pain through Clare's gut.

"They've given up," Clare whispered.

"Aye, they do feel defeated. But they still fight. They carry on. Look, look how he fights for you," the Goddess said, pointing to Blake screaming in fury as he destroyed Domnua after Domnua. "And there, your blonde friend. She fights through her tears. See how fierce she is?"

And she was fierce, Clare thought, tears in her eyes as she watched Bianca mow down another Domnua.

"Will they make it?" Clare asked, turning to look at the Goddess. "Please, I beg of you. Help them off the mountain."

"You'll have to help them yourself. You know where the stone is," the Goddess said gently and Clare gaped at her.

"I... what? I don't have the stone. I never found it. I failed," Clare whispered, frozen, blood dripping through her palms, still pressed to the wound in her chest.

"Then you didn't look hard enough," the Goddess said gently. "Remember the clues. And what the stone stands for."

Clare's mind whirled desperately as she pressed hard on her wound, her life's blood seeping from her.

Branna's face swam into her mind, an image of the day in her shop when she'd handed Clare a folded piece of paper.

"Though truth often varies, the heart never tarries, a stone is found, whence it is born."

"The truth," Clare gasped, thinking the riddle through and trying to piece everything together. "It's about love, isn't it?"

"Yes, it's about love," the Goddess agreed, doing nothing as Clare felt her soul begin to slip from her.

"The truth is that I love Blake. I love Bianca. And Seamus, and Branna, and all my family and friends. I love this country, living this life, and every piece of good in this world. The truth is that the stone is within my heart, isn't it?" Clare asked – and the Goddess beamed at her, her light multiplying a million times over, so that Clare had to shield her eyes with one bloody hand.

Suddenly, a song more beatific than a thousand angels singing came from inside her, and Clare felt a dull rip. She pulled her hand from her chest to see a brilliant blue stone, humming with energy and light, clasped in the bloodied fingers of her hand.

"The truth always lies in the heart," the Goddess said and then winked out of sight.

Clare felt detached for a moment, almost as if she were watching her body from above, and then she was falling.

In an instant, her senses returned, and she opened her

eyes to see herself back on the mountain in the middle of the battle, the lunar eclipse reversing itself and light beginning to shine once again.

Clare had landed, wholly healed, at a vantage point above her friends who still battled for their lives.

As she held the stone aloft, it began to sing – softly at first and then thundering down the mountain, a tidal wave of brilliant music, destroying every Domnua in its path. And as the music roared, the Danula cheered, the mountain shook and her friends froze, astonishment on their faces.

In seconds, the Domnua were nothing but silvery dust, and the Danula, golden-violet warriors by the hundreds, all knelt, saluting Clare and her friends. Then they turned as one, zipping down the mountain at superhuman speed and disappearing back to the place from whence they had come.

"Clare!" Bianca screamed, shattering the silence left in their wake.

"I'm alive," Clare screamed back. She tucked the stone safely into a leather pouch in her knapsack then began to run, half sliding, half falling her way down the mountain until she reached Bianca, almost bowling her over with her momentum.

In seconds, they were all holding onto each other, gasping, crying, and laughing, amazed they were alive.

"I thought you were dead. I saw you die," Bianca cried into Clare's neck.

"I did die. I think. Or I went to somewhere in between."

"How did you find the stone?" Bianca demanded, pulling back to look at her.

"Questions later," Blake said, reaching in and pulling Clare from Bianca's arms. Lifting her, he crushed his lips to hers – his kiss sharing all of the pent-up anguish and fear he'd felt when he'd seen her go over the ledge. Clare sobbed into his mouth, so desperately happy to be in his arms again.

"Blake, I love you. I think I've loved you since I first saw you. I should have said it. I shouldn't have been scared to tell you," Clare said, gasping against his lips, never wanting him to let her go.

"It doesn't matter. Shh, it doesn't matter now. I felt it. I knew," Blake said, smoothing a hand over her hair.

"No, but it does. That was the key, you see? Knowing my own truth. And owning it. I was the key all along," Clare murmured, and then closed her eyes as a wave of exhaustion took her under, her vision dulling at the edges.

"We need to get off this mountain," Blake said, immediately cradling Clare in his arms. "Can you guys make it?"

"Hell yeah, we can make it," Bianca crowed, and together they limped their way down the mountain, Blake carrying Clare the whole way as she passed in and out of consciousness.

The moon, shining brightly in the sky, having won its own battle against darkness, cheerfully lit their way.

"We're meant to go there," Clare insisted early the next morning. They'd caught a few hours' sleep back in the rooms that a joyous Cait had put them up in.

"How do you know that?" Blake demanded, hovering over Clare. He'd not let himself be a foot away from her since they'd come off the mountain.

"I just know," Clare said.

"Aye, the cove's great magick. I'm not surprised you're meant to go there," Cait agreed from where she sat sipping a cup of tea at the bar.

"See? Cait knows," Clare said stubbornly.

"Fine, we'll go to this cove. Then I'm taking you to Esther's so you can relax for at least a week," Blake said.

"I want to go! Can we go too? I want to learn a few of her recipes. It'll be a great holiday," Bianca gushed.

"Of course you're coming," Blake said, shaking his head at Bianca as she cheered.

After a fierce hug from Cait, and a detailed list of directions, they all piled back into the SUV and were soon cruising the curvy road that climbed the cliffs leading away from the small village of Grace's Cove.

"Lord, I can see why they live here. Though I think I'd miss the hustle and bustle of Dublin," Bianca said.

Clare silently agreed. The cliffs jutted so proudly into the sea, where gulls swooped and dived and many a poet probably dreamed. It was the place of fairytales, one that could easily claim your heart, Clare thought, as she absently rubbed a hand over her chest.

"Does it still hurt?" Blake asked, glancing over.

"Aye, it'll take a bit to heal," Clare admitted, though it mattered little to her. She'd felt the pain of mortal wounds, so this dull ache was nothing.

"I still can't believe the stone was inside you," Bianca marveled from the backseat.

"I'm not sure if it always was. But I think it needed a particular set of circumstances to manifest," Clare shrugged.

"It's gorgeous. What kind of stone is it?"

They'd all spent time examining the stone, though it had a tendency to sing in joy any time Clare held it, so they'd had to keep a wrap on it. But it was a perfectly formed sphere, glowing gently with an ethereal blue glow.

"I'd say there was some aquamarine in there, which is why my stones were made of that, but it's not all aquamarine," Clare said, running her finger over the ring she still wore on her finger. The necklace had been destroyed, but Clare was happy to have a small piece of this journey to keep with her always.

"This looks to be the place," Blake said, pulling the car over at a low stone wall. Further up the hill sat a small stone cottage with a cheerful red door, the foothills rising in a ridgeline behind.

"That must be Fiona's house," Bianca said as they got out of the car.

"Could you imagine living here? I mean, this view…" Seamus said, turning to look out over where the hills rolled off and fell sharply into the sea.

"Aye, I can see the appeal," Clare agreed. She happily took Blake's hand as they followed a worn path along the wall until it reached the edge of the cliff. Seamus let out a low whistle as they all looked down.

"That's pretty steep," Bianca said.

Two almost perfectly-formed cliffs arched out to form a large C, their points almost kissing each other in the middle, where water rushed in and out in gentle waves. A perfect sandy beach lay at the bottom; a path zigzagged from the top down to the beach.

"This would be perfect for a summer holiday," Bianca mused as they began the trek down.

"It's magick. You can't go here. Well, regular people can't just come here. The cove doesn't like it," Clare said over her shoulder. Silence met her words and she looked over her shoulder to see shocked faces.

"What? That's going to be the thing that weirds you out? After everything we've been through?"

"The lass has a point," Seamus agreed.

"Why is it charmed?" Bianca asked.

"The great Grace O'Malley died here. And she used powerful blood magick to protect her resting place, so when her daughter gave birth that very night upon this beach, more layers of magick were put in place."

"That *is* powerful magick," Bianca agreed.

"We've got to do a ritual, Cait said, before we get onto the beach," Clare said as they reached the bottom of the path, slightly out of breath.

"What happens if we don't?" Blake asked.

"I can't say I'm all that interested in finding out," Clare said, then pulled the necklace Branna had given her from around her neck. Stepping forward, she bent and drew a large circle in the sand with her finger and then motioned for everyone to step inside.

"We come in peace," Clare said, "We mean the cove no harm."

Though the words weren't fancy, Cait had told Clare that intent was all that mattered. And an offering. Clare hefted the necklace and threw it into the water, where it landed with a soft little plop.

"That's sad. Branna gave that to you," Bianca murmured.

"She'll find something else to give me. It doesn't matter what the gift is – just the thought behind it," Clare said, staring out at the waves.

"So, what now? Can we leave the circle?" Blake asked.

"We should be good, but…" Clare cocked her head and walked a little closer to the water, trying to see if her eyes were playing tricks on her.

"Is the water glowing?" Clare asked, as a soft blue light seemed to shimmer just under the surface.

"Aye, it's glowing."

A voice, like a thousand harps singing at once, flowed over them. They all threw their hands up to shield their eyes from the blinding light that came from a figure walking slowly toward them.

"It's the Goddess," Clare breathed, gripping Blake's arm. "The one who helped me."

"That's the Goddess Danu," Seamus said, dropping to his knees in the sand. Clare's mouth dropped open when Blake followed suit. Bianca and Clare looked at each other, unsure of what to do.

"Please, stand," Danu said, smiling at them.

"I believe I'm supposed to give you this?" Clare asked, reaching into her bag and holding out the stone. It immediately began to vibrate, an otherworldly song of beauty flowing from it – so emotional, so stunning, that tears streamed down Clare's face instantly.

"Yes, it's to return home. All the treasures will be returned to us once they are found, and we will protect them with great care forevermore," Danu said, gently taking the stone from Clare. As soon as it left Clare's hands, the song stopped, though light still whirled beautifully in the globe.

"You've honored your people this day," Danu said, stepping forward and laying her hand on Clare's chest where the wound still pained her. In seconds, a cool balm of healing washed over Clare's body, easing her pain.

"Thank you, your highness," Clare said awkwardly, unsure of how to address a goddess.

Danu threw back her head and laughed, the sound like a hundred bluebirds chirping.

"You'll be cared for, so long as you are on this plane. All of you," Danu said, looking at the four of them. "My gift to you – our thanks – is that we will watch over you and your loved ones. You've but to call on us for help when in need and we'll be there."

"That's a mighty gift," Blake breathed, bowing his head.

"A deserving one," Danu said. "Since you've finished your task early, which I'm quite proud of, you'll have a little time before you need to find the next Seeker."

"I… what?" Clare said, her eyes widening. She'd thought she was in the clear now.

"You'll need to find the next Seeker and help her on her way. There is only so much help we are allowed to give without violating the conditions of the curse," Danu said.

"Is that why, when I lay dying, you couldn't just tell me where the stone was?" Clare demanded.

"Aye, 'twas not my place. Nor within my power. Even I must abide by some rules," Danu said gently.

"Thank you for sending the Danula to help on the mountain," Bianca piped up and Danu smiled at her.

"And for you, my bravest of warrior friends, I have a gift and a task, should you accept it," Danu said, and Bianca's mouth dropped open.

"For me?" Bianca squeaked.

"Aye, for you," Danu said, holding out a golden necklace, an intricate pendant hanging from its strand. Bianca accepted it gratefully, her eyes huge as she looked up at Danu.

"This will give you the powers you need to help the others."

"The others? You want me to help the others?" Bianca breathed, her cheeks tinged with pink.

"You're a brilliant addition to a battle. Between your knowledge and your fierce spirit, you'll be nothing but an asset to the others. Should you choose to accept, of course," Danu said with a smile.

"Wait, but – you could get hurt," Clare began, and Bianca shot her a look.

"I'd be honored to help the others on their quest. Thank you for your trust in me," Bianca bowed and slipped the necklace over her head.

Clare bit her lip, worry for her friend rushing through her.

"Worry not, brave one." Danu smiled at Clare gently. "You'll be able to help Bianca – at least to find the next *Na Sirtheoir* and tell her of your tale."

"We need to find the next one?" Clare asked.

"Aye, you do. A name, then," Danu said as she slowly began to fade from view. "Sasha Flanagan."

And with that, she winked from sight, taking the Stone of Destiny with her.

Clare felt oddly bereft for a moment, as though a piece of herself was being lost forever – then she turned to look at the water, and gasped.

"The cove! It *is* glowing!"

Blake wrapped his arm around Clare and she leaned into him, while Seamus cuddled up to Bianca and pressed his lips to her neck. They watched the brilliant light show for a moment, appreciating the sheer beauty of the other-worldly light that shone from the water's depths.

"Cait told me that it glows in the presence of true love," Seamus said cheerfully.

Clare's heart did a funny little flip in her chest. She glanced at Bianca in time to see her friend's usually animated face showing nothing but pure shock, before she was surprised and distracted by Blake lifting and twirling her in a circle.

"Hear that, Doc? You were worth the wait."

I sincerely hope you enjoyed the first book in the Isle of Destiny series.

AS A FUN LITTLE bonus if you join my newsletter you can celebrate Christmas all year round with a trip back to

Grace's Cove. As a welcome gift, I will send you a digital copy of Wild Irish Christmas right to your inbox. Use the link or scan the QR code to get your copy today.

https://offer.triciaomalley.com/free

READERS ARE RAVING about this feel-good novella where the worlds of Isle of Destiny and the Mystic Cove meet. And don't worry - fan favorites Bianca & Seamus make an appearance!

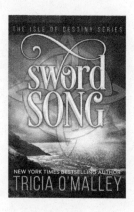

The Isle of Destiny Series, Book 2- Available now as an e-book, paperback or audiobook!

Sign up for information on new releases, free books, and fun giveaways at my website www.triciaomalley.com

---

The following is an excerpt from Sword Song

Book 2 in The Isle of Destiny Series

CHAPTER 1

"*A*nother one of you? You're getting to be quite the little pests," Sasha Flanagan swore as she circled a silver-eyed man whose unblinking stare never left her face. His body coiled like a spring as he watched her every move, waiting to pounce.

Deciding to ruffle his feathers a little, Sasha dipped forward and lashed out with a lithe iron sword she'd fashioned for just such occasions. Pleased to see the silver-eyed man jump back, she pushed forward.

"I don't know where you come from. Or what you want with me – but you'll be taking a message home to your friends," Sasha said, darting forward again and was rewarded with a yelp of pain from the man as the blade sliced neatly down his side. A trickle of silver seeped from him and he glared at her.

"Either I kill you now or you walk away and tell your buddies to leave me alone," Sasha said easily, her eyes tracking his every feint, waiting for the subtle hint that would telescope his next move.

And seeing it, she slid her blade neatly through the man's heart, grimacing as he dissolved in a silvery puddle on the pavement in the alleyway behind her gallery.

She'd gotten used to taking her blade everywhere with her.

One of these days, she hoped to figure out why she was being targeted by the fae, but for now, survival came first.

With a sigh, Sasha flicked her long, straight black hair over her shoulder and picked up the trash bag from where she'd dropped it when she'd first come outside. Tossing it into the dumpster, she walked backwards to the door of her gallery before slipping inside and locking up behind her.

Triple locks, iron bound, and a security alarm.

It wasn't just for the fae, but also for the valuables she housed here.

Cloak & Dagger was Sasha's pride and joy and was far more than just a traditional gallery. With a focus on antiquities and weaponry from every era, it housed one of the largest collections of ornate and intricately designed swords and daggers in all of Europe.

She couldn't quite say when her obsession with sharp instruments had come into play exactly. It could have been the time her father found her dancing on the counter with a knife in hand at the tender age of four. Or it might have been when she discovered her first fencing book and taught herself with a thin stick behind the wall of the garden.

Sasha smiled as she slipped her blade into the sheath at her belt. She still remembered the first time she'd slid the foil out and brandished it in front of her. Instantly, there had been a recognition – an understanding – that she was born to wield a weapon.

What followed that had been a strict study of martial arts, fencing, swordplay and finally, an intense regimen of studies that had taken her across Europe to study ancient weaponry. Her good looks, combined with no-nonsense manner, had opened more than one art collector's door.

And by the tender age of thirty, she'd opened her own store and become one of the leading experts in Celtic and Roman weaponry in Ireland, if not in the world.

One would think her prowess with a sword would have given her fiancé pause before he cheated on her.

Sasha rolled her eyes as she crossed the honey-toned wood floors of her gallery to flick the lights off in the front display windows. Pulling down her metal protective gate that secured the windows at night, she locked them and turned to look at her gallery.

Aaron had never appreciated what she'd built here.

A cool grey color covered the walls, just a hint darker than white, allowing the colors of the swords and daggers on display to pop. Sasha had created little collection areas that would walk a visitor through various eras of weaponry. The display was stunning and her store was one of her greatest accomplishments, if she didn't say so herself.

Aaron had sniffed at it and referred to her gallery as

"Sasha's little folly." Sasha rolled her eyes again as she crossed the room, switching off lights as she went. Her hand unconsciously went to the knife sheathed at her waist as she remembered the day she'd come home early to surprise Aaron and make him a home-cooked meal for once.

Sasha huffed out a laugh.

It was all so trite and boring, really. Same old story. Finding your lover in bed with someone else, Sasha thought, as she sat at her desk and switched her laptop on.

Cheating was a coward's way out. And the last thing Sasha needed was to be hitched to a lazy cheater. It had been a blessing in disguise, though at the time, Sasha had barely restrained herself from taking a knife to his unmentionables. And she did mean unmentionable, Sasha snorted.

Not that she hadn't threatened it.

The very real fear in his eyes had been enough to tame the beast inside of Sasha, and she'd kicked him out that very day, and hadn't had to see him since. She couldn't say that the experience had done anything to increase her willingness to trust other people again –but she was working on it.

It didn't help that silver-eyed fae had begun popping up everywhere she went and had been trying to kill her. That'll do something for a person's trust – in pretty much everything and anyone.

Sasha leaned in and began to read an email she'd received from a contact she'd reached out to. For a month now, she'd been trying to dig deeper into the history of the fae in Ireland and how legend wove into reality. Separating fact from fiction was an almost insurmountable task, but she was chipping away at it a day at a time.

And the reality of it was – fae existed and they were trying to kill her.

It was enough to keep her up all night as she sought answers.

Available in audio, e-book & paperback!
<u>Available from Amazon</u>

ALSO BY TRICIA O'MALLEY

THE ISLE OF DESTINY SERIES

Stone Song

Sword Song

Spear Song

Sphere Song

A completed series in Kindle Unlimited.

Available in audio, e-book & paperback!

"Love this series. I will read this multiple times. Keeps you on the edge of your seat. It has action, excitement and romance all in one series."

- Amazon Review

THE ENCHANTED HIGHLANDS

Wild Scottish Knight

Wild Scottish Love

Wild Scottish Rose

"I love everything Tricia O'Malley has ever written and "Wild Scottish Knight" is no exception. The new setting for this magical journey is Scotland, the home of her new husband and soulmate. Tricia's love for her husbands country shows in every word she writes. I have always wanted to visit Scotland but have never had the time and money. Having read "Wild Scottish Knight" I feel I have begun to to experience Scotland in a way few see it. I am ready to go see Loren Brae, the castle and all its magical creatures, for myself. Tricia O'Malley makes the fantasy world of Loren Brae seem real enough to touch!"

-Amazon Review

Available in audio, e-book, hardback, paperback and is included in your Kindle Unlimited subscription.

THE WILDSONG SERIES

Song of the Fae

Melody of Flame

Chorus of Ashes

Lyric of Wind

"The magic of Fae is so believable. I read these books in one sitting and can't wait for the next one. These are books you will reread many times."

- Amazon Review

A completed series in Kindle Unlimited.

Available in audio, e-book & paperback!

A completed series in Kindle Unlimited.

Available in audio, e-book & paperback!

"Love her books and was excited for a totally new and different one! Once again, she did NOT disappoint! Magical in multiple ways and on multiple levels. Her writing style, while similar to that of Nora Roberts, kicks it up a notch!! I want to visit that island, stay in the B&B and meet the gals who run it! The characters are THAT real!!!" - Amazon Review

THE ALTHEA ROSE SERIES

One Tequila

Tequila for Two

Tequila Will Kill Ya (Novella)

Three Tequilas

Tequila Shots & Valentine Knots (Novella)

Tequila Four

A Fifth of Tequila

A Sixer of Tequila

Seven Deadly Tequilas

Eight Ways to Tequila

Tequila for Christmas (Novella)

"Not my usual genre but couldn't resist the Florida Keys setting. I was hooked from the first page. A fun read with just the right amount of crazy! Will definitely follow this series."- Amazon Review

A completed series in Kindle Unlimited.

Available in audio, e-book & paperback!

THE MYSTIC COVE SERIES

Wild Irish Heart

Wild Irish Eyes

Wild Irish Soul

Wild Irish Rebel

Wild Irish Roots: Margaret & Sean

Wild Irish Witch

Wild Irish Grace

Wild Irish Dreamer

Wild Irish Christmas (Novella)

Wild Irish Sage

Wild Irish Renegade

Wild Irish Moon

"I have read thousands of books and a fair percentage have been romances. Until I read Wild Irish Heart, I never had a book actually make me believe in love."- Amazon Review

A completed series in Kindle Unlimited.

Available in audio, e-book & paperback!

STAND ALONE NOVELS

Ms. Bitch

"Ms. Bitch is sunshine in a book! An uplifting story of fighting your way through heartbreak and making your own version of happily-ever-after."

~Ann Charles, USA Today Bestselling Author

Starting Over Scottish

Grumpy. Meet Sunshine.

She's American. He's Scottish. She's looking for a fresh start. He's returning to rediscover his roots.

One Way Ticket

A funny and captivating beach read where booking a one-way ticket to paradise means starting over, letting go, and taking a chance on love…one more time

10 out of 10 - The BookLife Prize

CONTACT ME

I hope my books have added a little magick into your life. If you have a moment to add some to my day, you can help by telling your friends and leaving a review. Word-of-mouth is the most powerful way to share my stories. Thank you.

Love books? What about fun giveaways? Nope? Okay, can I entice you with underwater photos and cute dogs? Let's stay friends, receive my emails and contact me by signing up at my website

www.triciaomalley.com

Or find me on Facebook and Instagram.
@triciaomalleyauthor

Made in the USA
Las Vegas, NV
15 July 2023

74769999R00173